the Christmas
MISTAKE

Darcy Rose

USA Today Bestselling Author

Frankie Barrymore. 20.

101 15ᵗʰ Street, apartment 8.

Twenty thousand dollars.

"Hey. This should be an easy one." I hand the burner phone I use to access the job posting board to my brother, Evan. My partner in our little business. "Twenty-year-old kid? Against the two of us? We'd make it to the bar in time for last call."

Not that we go to the bar after completing a job. It's as much of a joke as my brother and I have—there isn't a ton of laughter in our world unless one of us is laughing at the other. The first time we pulled a job, we made sure to get out of there early enough to get to the corner bar in time for last call. The idea was to be seen by the regulars there, people who recognized us. An alibi, in other words.

We were so fucking green back then.

We were also pulling robberies. Small-time shit we don't even bother with anymore. We've moved up in the world —or down, depending on how you look at it.

Evan frowns, scanning the screen. "Twenty years old. Somebody's kid, and we're taking him out a few days before Christmas? That's cold."

That makes me snort. "It's gonna be Christmas for us with a fat paycheck under the tree. Besides, how many jobs did you pull by that age?"

"Good point." He scrubs a hand over his short black hair. Like nearly everything else about us, mine is the same. We could be twins if it wasn't for the two years between us and the thin scar running from Evan's temple to his jaw. "But that's us. Not everybody had to do the shit we did when we were that age."

"He must have done something to piss someone off enough to call a hit for twenty grand. I doubt this guy is a saint. It doesn't matter, either way. Are we in or not?" I take the phone back, brows lifted as I wait for an answer. "Twenty thousand for a quick in-and-out job. We've done a lot worse."

"Yeah, sure." He shrugs it off. I click the button indicating we'll take the job. It's as easy as that. The job will be easy, too. Killing a twenty-year-old kid. Maybe he had a future ahead of him, maybe not. All I know is, somebody with money wants him dead.

Usually, we get people involved with the wrong crowd—owing someone money, losing a bet, even the occasional revenge kill. Also hot on the hit list are disgruntled business partners, who usually live in nicer houses or apartments. Sometimes it's a cheating husband whose wife got sick of his bullshit. Sometimes it's the husband who wants the wife dead—or a girlfriend who refuses to keep her mouth shut.

That part, we usually find out while doing reconnaissance before going in for the hit. But there aren't any bells and whistles to this one. Nothing to indicate this is somebody important, with ties to the underworld or in a house with a complex security system. No warnings whatsoever. I wish they were all this easy.

101 15th Street. Shitty neighborhood. No chance of a security system there. What could they have to protect? This is looking better all the time. Good thing I happened to check the new job listings when I did, or somebody else could be getting ready to take advantage.

On the way into town, I can't help but wonder about Frankie Barrymore. Who is he? Who'd he piss off? Living in a dump like the one now coming into view, either he's a lowlife wannabe criminal or a dumb kid who happened to be in the wrong place at the wrong time. I shouldn't think about him at all, really—no sense humanizing somebody who's only going to breathe air for the next twenty minutes or so—but a part of me always wonders. What does a person have to do to get his name listed on those boards? Does he have any idea we're coming for him?

I hope he's sleeping well and having good dreams. Maybe he'll get lucky, and we'll embed a couple of bullets in his brain while he's dreaming. Maybe he'll stay wherever he is and never know he's dead.

My brain's all fucked tonight. Evan notices, too, grunting in my general direction as he turns onto 15th. "What's with you? You'd think we were on our way to a funeral."

I only roll my eyes, focusing my attention on the corner apartment building. It's amazing the thing's still standing. I guess rat turds are stronger than they look since the foundation must be built on them.

Evan parks half a block down. No worries about whether we'll be noticed since the streetlights are broken. The city must not see fit to come out and replace them. Works for me. A handful of random people lurk in those shadows, hanging out in doorways and sleeping in alleys. We're night people, like they are. They know better than to pay attention to what happens out here, and so do we. There's no threat from them.

The night air is cold as my brother and I walk quickly from the car, a beat-up old rust bucket we use for jobs like this, to the corner building. One of the apartment windows holds blinking Christmas lights, reminding me the holiday is tomorrow. Something about those lights strikes me as sad. Like whoever put them up has hope even though they live here.

The apartment is on the third floor. The hall smells just as much like piss and despair as I figured. Evan's nose wrinkles in disgust when we come to a stop at the door, where he looks over his shoulder before checking his Glock. I do the same while listening for sounds of life coming from inside the apartment. There's no light visible under the door. No sound, either.

And the lock's a joke. If I lived somewhere like this, you'd better believe I'd have more than a doorknob lock. All it takes is a credit card, and I'm inside the dark, silent shoebox of a home.

In and out. That's all we need. And if he's not home yet, we can stick around until he shows up. I hope he doesn't take long since I don't love being here. A baby wails from a couple of doors down, and somewhere else, a woman weeps. I drown both sounds out. It reminds me too much of my childhood.

Evan leads the way down a narrow hall, past a tiny living room and a kitchen that looks like it hasn't been updated in a few decades. A faint light shines from inside the room at the end of the hall, where the door's partly open.

No need to check in with each other before moving forward. We've been through this too many times before. Evan takes the lead with me right behind him. It strikes me that Frankie may not be alone—well, that's a shame for whoever she is, hooking up with a guy who has a price on his head.

The door opens silently when Evan lifts it slightly on its hinges. I don't know what I expected to find in the bedroom. A kid lying on a bare mattress, alone or other- wise? Something as bleak as the rest of the apartment, the rest of the building?

Instead, the bed is draped in pink. Pillows, duvet, the whole nine yards. The light I saw coming from under the door is courtesy of the blinking Christmas lights in the window behind a gauzy curtain.

Son of a bitch.

It's a little girl's bedroom.

Only the person in the bed is no little girl. She's a full-grown woman with shiny dark hair spread over the pillow like a fan. She sleeps with a hand on the pillow next to her face. What a face, too. Gorgeous, peaceful, glowing.

Fuck, we're in the wrong apartment. One look at Evan shows me he's just as stunned as me. This never happens. People don't give us the wrong address when they want someone dead. This is not a pizza delivery. It's a death sentence.

"Maybe this is his sister or girlfriend," I whisper more to myself, but in the quiet room, my brother hears me just fine.

"There." He points at something in the corner of the room. "Check her purse."

Looking at where Evan is pointing, I find a purse propped up on a chair. I silently cross the room and fish her wallet out of her worn purse. Flipping it open, I search for her ID.

"Motherfucker," I curse when I see the name next to the girl's picture. "Frances Barrymore. It's her; she is Frankie."

"Well, fuck."

Frankie. That's a guy's name. Nobody would think they were going to a girl's apartment when they read that name. But the person in bed is most definitely a girl, and she looks awfully at home. This is her bedroom, her bed. Her apartment.

I nod to the door, and Evan takes the hint. Once we're out in the hall, we turn to each other. "What the fuck?" he whispers while staring at the bed.

"How should I know?" He's talking to me like I did this on purpose. "I'm lost here, too."

One thing I don't think either of us is lost on: we took the job. There's no getting out of it. No returns policy. The girl has to die. "It'll be better to get it over with fast," Evan points out. "Before she wakes up."

He's right. I know he's right. That doesn't mean I have to like it.

I don't even know why I don't like it. We've killed women before. It's not my favorite, but a job's a job. Money's money. We're providing a service. There's nothing different about this.

So why can't I go the fuck in there and pull the trigger? He's right. It'll be better to get it done fast. A mercy. There are sick fucks out there—sicker than us—who would get off on finding a girl in bed instead of a guy. They'd put it in her ass first, then kill her. Sort of a bonus.

Why isn't this making me feel any better?

"Come on." Evan nudges me. "We gotta do it."

"I know." I nudge him back. Pretty soon, nudges are going to turn into something worse, and the girl will wake up because we're beating the hell out of each other outside her bedroom door.

"So?"

"So if you're in such a hurry, go in there and do it yourself." I shrug. "Go ahead."

His eyes narrow in a dangerous way. If I didn't know better, I'd think he was considering putting a bullet in my head instead of the girl in the other room. Sleeping in that girlie bed. "Don't pull that reverse psychology shit with me."

"Who says I am?" I should go in there. I know I should, but I can't make my feet move. Not when she's sleeping so peacefully. When she's tempting me with all those curves under that pink blanket. Not where my head should be right now, not even close, but nothing about any of this makes sense.

"We have to do this. She won't even know. Look around this place. It's not like she has a great life, and she must have done something to end up on that list. We're probably doing her a favor taking her out in her sleep." Right, and wasn't I just thinking that back in the car? She'll get lucky and end up staying in the dream she's in now. Judging by the way she's sleeping—like a rock—it's not a nightmare. Good for her.

He's right. I know he's right. That's why I take a deep breath and go back in there, back to the bed. I stand beside it, staring down at her. *Sorry, Frankie. You pissed off the wrong person.* Though I can't imagine how an angel like this could piss anybody off. Not to the point where they'd pay twenty grand to have her killed.

Evan stands on the other side of the bed, across from me. We exchange one last look. A nod. We're ready to do what has to be done. Maybe.

And that's when she wakes up. Her eyes fly open and connect with mine like two magnets drawn to each other. There is a small moment before her fear takes over, where she just looks at me. Not quite awake but not asleep. Her big baby-blue eyes just stare at me, and I'm not sure what's happening. It's like the world around us stands still. My chest feels funny, warm, and fuzzy. I've never experienced anything like it, but I already know I won't kill her, and neither will Evan.

Because not only won't I hurt her but no one else will. They'll have to go through me first.

FRANKIE

*W*hat the—?

For a second, it's like I'm still sleeping. There's no way these two guys are actually standing at my bedside. The only place in the world where I feel safe and whole. Yes, I'm still sleeping in the same bed and bedding I had when I was a little girl. It's the only thing I have left. I've never even let anyone in my bedroom before.

But they are. I'm awake, and the two of them are clear as day with multicolored lights blinking, shining on their faces. It's like a surreal nightmare.

I suck in a breath, ready to scream—what else am I supposed to do?—but one of them clamps a hand over my mouth before I can do anything. I claw at his wrist, kicking when the other one tries to grab my legs. It doesn't make a difference how hard I fight. They're both too strong.

Too strong for me to defend myself. Two of them against one of me. Terror turns my blood to ice while a hundred ugly, painful images race through my brain all at once.

"Stop fighting," one of them growls over my muffled screams. "I said fucking stop." I don't even know which of them is speaking. I don't know anything but fear. The hand over my mouth tightens, no matter how I claw at it. Instead of that, I punch the inside of his elbow to make his arm go weak long enough to twist my head and get my mouth free.

"What are you doing here?" It's a stupid question. It's obvious what they're doing here. I'm about to scream again, but the one I punched covers my mouth again, and this time, his fingers press into my face hard enough to bring tears to my eyes.

"Stop, Frankie. You're only going to hurt yourself." The one holding my body still sits on the edge of the bed. He has a gun. They both do. They're here to kill me. "You're wasting your time."

"Who sent you here? Why are you here?" I try to wiggle away because, honestly, what else am I going to do? Lie here and take it? How do they know my name?

They ignore me, looking at each other instead. They have to be brothers. They look too much alike to be anything else. And they're having a silent conversation. Finally, it's too much, and I start fighting again. I'm kicking and punching harder this time, and it's almost enough to get me out of bed.

Until one of them grabs me by the waist. "Fine. This is how it's going to have to be." He throws me back onto the bed, my face pressed against the mattress while the other one leaves the bedroom. He's back in what feels like seconds later, and I hear the sound of tape being ripped from a roll.

No matter how I struggle, they manage to tape my wrists together behind me. My ankles come next. Tears are running down my face when they roll me onto my back.

One of them reaches out for me, and I flinch away, but all he does is wipe a tear from my cheek with his thumb. If he hadn't bound me thirty seconds ago, the gesture would almost be sweet.

"Please, don't—" The rest of my plea is lost when a big piece of tape covers my mouth.

They're arguing with each other, the two of them muttering in low voices. One of them walks out of the room while the other one carries me over his shoulder.

"Don't even think about kicking me," he warns. "We're not always nice guys. Don't push us too far." I get the feeling he's telling the truth. But what are they doing to me? Where are we going? All I can do is mumble my questions behind the tape.

Before long, we're outside in the cold. I'm placed into the back seat of a car that the other guy must have pulled up in front of my building so they wouldn't have to carry me too far. Have they done this before? They must have since it seems like they have this down to a science.

Though I don't think I was part of their plan. They're too flustered and arguing with each other. The question is, if they didn't come to kidnap me, what did they come here to do?

They mutter to each other almost nonstop as we roll away from my building and head down the street. What was it I heard once? If a victim is moved to another location, it's pretty much guaranteed they're going to die. That's robberies, though. Does that count now? What the hell am I even thinking? I need to get my head together. If I'm panicking, I can't get away.

They didn't give me any room to wiggle my arms or legs. I remember seeing a video once, instructions on how to get out of duct tape. But my hands are behind me, so I can't use that. What else do I know? Think, think, I have to think. Even if it seems pointless and useless because there are two of them and only one of me. They're so much bigger and stronger.

And they have guns. I've never had a gun pointed at me before. Guess I can cross that off my bucket list.

There's no reason to laugh right now, but one tries to work its way out of my chest anyway. The sound doesn't get far, thanks to the tape over my mouth. My tears have seeped into it, enough that it's starting to come loose at one corner. I rub my face against the seat and try to pull more of it back. If I can talk, maybe I can get through to them.

I know it's pointless, but I have to do something. I'm not going to die without at least trying to save myself.

The tape's maybe a quarter of the way loose when we come to a sudden stop, the driver hitting the brakes hard enough that I almost roll off the seat. For one second, I think maybe there's a cop out there on the street, and we almost ran a light. Maybe that's why. Maybe I can scream and get their attention.

No such luck. My heart sinks when both men open their doors and continue their tense conversation outside the car. Before I can calm my racing heart enough to hear what they're saying, the back door near my feet opens, and a pair of hands close around my ankles, yanking me out of the car.

We've arrived.

All I manage to get a glimpse of is a house. A nice house, too, the kind of place I used to dream about living in when I was a kid. Before I knew better, back when I thought anything was possible. I turn my head as much as I can, trying to get a feel of the surroundings, but all I see are trees and more trees. We're in the middle of nowhere.

They've brought me out to the middle of nowhere. Nobody will hear me screaming. Panic floods me again, fresh and new, and I can't help but wiggle and thrash in the arms of the man carrying me.

"Knock it the fuck off." It's a growl, low and threatening. "You're already more trouble than you're worth."

"Shut up, Evan," the other one says. Evan, at least I know one of their names. The other guy opens the door, looking around like he wants to make sure we're alone while his brother carries me into the house.

It's nice inside, too. The living room is off the entry, and that's where my kidnapper drops me, right onto a sectional sofa set up across from a widescreen TV mounted on the wall. I almost bounce onto the floor, he drops me so hard. "This is fucking ridiculous." He glares down at me, and I notice a scar running down the left side of his face. It's not big or even ugly, but it makes him look scarier than ever.

The way he looms over me isn't helping things.

His brother joins him after flipping on a lamp. This one doesn't have a scar, but he's wearing the same hard, angry look. "We're in it now," he grunts. "No going back."

I want to tell them they can go back. They absolutely can. All that comes out is muffled groans, though.

The one without the scar grimaces. "If you promise not to scream, I'll take the tape off your mouth."

"Not that screaming will help anything," his brother warns. "There's nobody around for a mile in any direction. At least."

"All it'll do is piss us off, and you don't want to do that." He leans down, takes hold of the tape, and pulls it away. I can't help whimpering in pain, but at least I can breathe better now.

"Why?" It's the biggest question looming in my mind. "Why are you doing this? Why me?"

"You really don't know?" They exchange a look.

"No." There are tears in my eyes, in my voice. I can't help it. I don't want to be weak, to let them think it'll be easy to do whatever they want to me, but what else am I supposed to do? My whole life is flashing in front of me.

"We've gotta do something with her." Evan scrubs a hand over his black hair. "Right?"

"Obviously."

"Don't hurt me. Please." I know it sounds pitiful, and it's what people in this position probably always say, but it's the only thing that comes to mind. "Whatever this is about, we can figure it out. I know we can."

I try to move my legs, but they're starting to cramp. My groan isn't for show. "Can you get rid of the tape, please? It's hurting me."

They have another one of those silent conversations, staring at each other. Evan snorts like he's not a fan of the idea, but his brother sits on the edge of the couch anyway and pulls something out of his back pocket.

"Relax." He rolls his eyes when I gasp. "How else do you want me to get it off?" He opens the knife and works it under the tape on my ankles until he can peel it free. Only his hand rests on my ankles longer than it needs to, then starts inching up my calf.

I pull it away, and he only snickers before giving the same treatment to the tape around my wrists. My muscles ache enough to make me whimper again when the blood starts flowing, but it means I'm free. Free-ish, anyway.

Neither of them stops me when I work my way into a sitting position, then draw my knees up to my chest and wrap my arms around them. I'm only wearing a long T-shirt, but it covers most of me when I pull it over my legs, of all the nights to go to bed without at least shorts on.

The rest of the house is silent. It's just the three of us. "Why did you bring me here?" I ask in a whisper. I don't know whether I want the answer. "Who are you?"

"Who are we?" They exchange a look. "Right now, we're the reason you're still alive."

EVAN

This is a fucking mistake. All the way around. No other way to describe it.

But the alternative is somehow worse.

I don't know what it is about her, but Mason feels it, too. Or else the girl would be dead in her bed right now, and we'd be... well, we'd be here, probably. Without her. Without guilt or remorse or any of that shit.

So why couldn't we go through with it?

And why do I want to touch her so badly? Goddamn, she's tempting. Now that I've gotten a feel of her smooth skin— like silk—I want more.

"My name's Evan." I jerk my chin at my brother. "That's Mason. And I hate to be the one to break it to you, but we were sent to your apartment to kill you."

She gasps, flinching like I hurt her. Mason groans. "Nice. Make sure you scare the shit out of her."

"I think it's too late for that. What's the point of pretending? Somebody wants her dead, and we were sent there to make it happen."

"Why would anybody want me dead?" She sounds like a little girl, which makes sense considering the sort of bed she sleeps in. If it hadn't been for that princess setup and the Christmas lights and all that, this might've turned out differently. Something about it was enough to make me think twice. To hesitate. I never hesitate if I can help it. That's the sort of shit that can get a person killed.

But this time, there was no helping it. I couldn't make myself pull the trigger. Then she woke up, and it only took one look at those baby blue eyes to tuck away my gun.

"We don't know why. We just take the job. No questions asked," Mason explains, folding his arms. "You tell us. Who did you fuck over?"

"I have no idea. I mean it." Her eyes dart back and forth between us. Beautiful innocent eyes. The pale blue is offset by her dark hair and creamy skin, but right now, they're huge and full of fear. "It must've been some kind of mistake. You had the wrong apartment."

"So how come I know your name, Frankie Barrymore?"

She flinches, pulling her legs closer to her chest. It would take no effort at all to spread those thighs and see what's going on under that shirt she's wearing. It's thin enough that I'd be able to see her nipples through it if her legs weren't in the way.

Her eyes go round, widening until they practically bulge from her head. "But… why?"

"We're not the ones who can answer that question. And honestly, it doesn't matter right now."

"To you, maybe."

Mason breaks in before I can remind her that we're doing her a favor and don't want to hear her smart mouth. There's plenty I could do with that mouth. I doubt she'd like all of it—at least, not right away. She'd tell herself she didn't, of course. "What matters now is keeping you out of sight. So they think you're dead."

It takes her a second to catch on. I guess I'd be confused, too, if I woke up with two strangers pointing guns at me. All in all, she's handling it pretty well.

"So I'm supposed to hide for the rest of my life? I can't ever go home?" She gulps. "Not ever?"

"Why would you want to?" Mason shoots me a look for that, but I don't much care. I'm genuinely surprised she would feel this way. "I mean, I was there. I saw what your life looked like. If anything, this is a second chance."

"A second chance at what?" A disbelieving little giggle bubbles up from her chest. "With what? Using what? I don't even have an ID now. It's all at the apartment. I have to go back for it."

"No. You can't."

"But I have to!"

I hate complaining more than just about anything else. "Okay, quit the whining." I have to get up and put space between us, or else I don't know what I'll do. She might look like a woman, but she's acting like a spoiled little brat. Maybe she just needs a spanking.

Mason's always had more patience than me. "You just can't. They'll know you're alive, whoever they are. Which means they'll be even more determined to find you and get rid of you for real. Understand?"

She starts rocking back and forth, staring straight ahead with her chin on her knees. For a second, I think she might be in shock. I mean, I guess I would be, too. Mason and I look at each other. He lifts a shoulder.

"I have to use the bathroom. Now. I'm going to be sick." She gets up, swaying a little. I reach out and catch her before she hits the floor, meaning she lands against me. It might've been better to let her drop since having her warm, soft body in my arms sets off all kinds of dark, nasty thoughts.

But the idea of having puke all over me isn't a turn-on, so I steer her to the bathroom on this floor. "Just breathe," I mutter, practically carrying her when her legs don't work fast enough. "Don't throw up on me." She stumbles into the room, and I close the door before I have to see anything. Hearing her gagging is bad enough.

I can blow a guy's brains out without flinching. But puke is too much.

Mason sighs, rubbing the back of his neck. "This is a bad idea."

"No shit." I press in on my temples, trying to ward off a headache. "But what do you want to do about it? Take her back? This was your idea, remember?"

"Fuck you. You went along with it. It's not like you were about to pull the trigger, either."

He's right. I could've ended this pretty easily. Squeeze the trigger, problem solved. Extra money to grab a few more Christmas gifts for Mom. She always did love Christmas —even more than we did when we were kids. At least it seemed that way.

Now? A girl is throwing up in my bathroom, and we have to make it look like we killed her. Add in how fucking tempting she is, and this is a recipe for disaster.

Thinking of her brings my attention back to the closed door. She's not gagging anymore. "You okay in there? We've got things to discuss." No answer.

Shit. I look at Mason, who's staring at the door. "Frankie? Say something."

"Are there razors or pills in there?" I turn the knob and find she locked the door at some point. When did that happen? How did I miss it? "Dammit, Frankie, don't make me break this door down. You'll be the one who ends up paying for it."

When I don't get an answer, there's no choice but to kick the damn thing down. It doesn't take much effort. The door swings open, wood splinters flying.

And there she is, with her ass hanging out of the window, the top half of her body outside. Trying to get away. "Are you fucking with me?" Before I know what I'm doing, I cross the room and slap her across the ass, good and hard. I don't know what made me do it. The feeling of dealing with an ignorant little brat, maybe. Brats get spanked.

She jumps a little, kicking out with her feet. "Don't hurt me, please! Don't hurt me!"

"Nobody *was* going to hurt you." Now, though? Now I want to teach her a lesson. First, I have to get her out of the window, where she got herself stuck. "We should leave you like this and let you freeze to death, you fucking idiot." A couple of tugs, and she's back in the room, sliding down the wall until she crouches on the floor with her arms crossed over her bent head.

"Please. Just let me go." She's shaking from head to toe, and I don't think it's from the cold. Something about the way she's acting makes my blood boil. We saved her life tonight, and she's acting like we're the ones who ordered the hit on her.

Trying to get away only pisses me the fuck off. If she sent the cops our way, we would have to move again. I'm mad thinking about how her actions could have fucked us over. All it does is make me want to hurt her. To give her something to cry about.

"How far did you think you were going to get?" Mason demands, standing beside me and looking just as pissed as

I feel. "You're barefoot and practically naked. It's like thirty degrees out there."

"Let me go, please." She repeats so quietly, I can barely hear her. "I'll run away. I'll make myself disappear."

"Yeah, right." Bending down, I take her by the waist, lifting her up and throwing her over my shoulder. She flops like a rag doll. "You have the money to make yourself disappear? Tell me another good one."

"What are you doing?" She squirms when I start up the stairs, heading for my bedroom.

"I'm making sure you don't get any other smart ideas about running away."

"No. No!" Her fighting gets worse when she realizes where we're going. Once we're in the room, I flip on the lights before dumping her on the bed. She scrambles around, trying to get away, but the sight of Mason standing in the doorway stops her. She knows she's trapped.

There are neckties in the closet. Gifts from a long time ago, gifts Mom thought I'd enjoy. Granted, she believed her sons worked in an office someplace, so it was only natural she would try to outfit us on our birthdays and at Christmas. They've never been used.

Until now. Until I tie Frankie's wrists to the headboard, pulling the silk tight enough to make her wince. Something about the sight and sound of that makes my cock twitch. Her arms are above her head, hands resting on the pillow. She's completely helpless now.

I lean over her, taking in the scent of the shampoo she uses and the faint perspiration she's managed to work up. "Wasn't it better when we didn't have to tie you up? You brought this on yourself." She tries to turn away from me, but it's no use. She's trapped. Her thin T-shirt shifts a little, riding up on her thighs and brushing over her taut nipples. Hunger unfurls deep in my core. "I'm not gonna lie, though. I like you tied up like this."

A shiver runs down her body. And she thought she had something to be scared of before.

One glance at my brother tells me he's thinking along the same lines—he's breathing harder, nostrils flared, gaze fixed on Frankie's delicious body. She's doing the same thing to him she's doing to me without meaning to. Enticing. Teasing.

"Please… don't do this," she begs so sweetly, not knowing the kind of pleasure we could bring her. She is afraid, in shock, but we could make it good for her. I could definitely convince her body.

My cock might be ready, but the rest of me needs sleep and time to think. I need to figure out what we're supposed to do with her now that she's here, so I kick off my shoes and stretch out next to Frankie on the king-sized bed. When she tries to squirm away again, she gets a surprise in the form of Mason, who's doing the same as I am. She's not just trapped. She's sandwiched between us.

"Relax," I mutter, closing my eyes. "If you didn't try to get away, this wouldn't be happening. We can't trust you now."

"I won't ever try again. I swear." Her head swings back and forth between us. "Please, don't make me do this."

"All you had to do was behave yourself." Mason snickers when she whimpers at the touch of his fingers against her cheek. "Chill out. You might end up enjoying your time with us."

"I doubt it. I'm scared," she admits.

"You should be, but not of us. You should be scared of the guy who ordered the hit. And right now, we're the only people standing in his way."

Scrunching her eyebrows together, she looks conflicted, probably trying to figure out if she can trust anything we are saying. "If all of that is true, why are you protecting me?"

"Once we saw you in your princess bed, we couldn't kill you. You were just too cute, too innocent, too tempting."

"You want me for sex?" she asks directly.

"Yes," I admit shamelessly.

"I bet you didn't put this on your list to Santa," Mason adds.

I'm still grinning at his joke as I settle my head onto my pillow. "Don't worry, doll. Right now, we're just sleeping. Try to catch some, too."

I close my eyes, and it doesn't take me long to fall asleep, and Frankie's soft whimpers fade to silence.

*W*hat do I do now?

There's no getting away. Not with one of them on either side of me. I'm not even sure they're sleeping. What if this is a test to see how I'll handle things?

I can't move my hands, and my arms hurt from being over my head for hours. How am I supposed to sleep? Then again, I don't think I'd be sleeping anyway. There's too much to think about and be afraid of. What are they going to want once they're awake? I saw the way they both looked at me, especially when Evan tied me up. They want me, and I'm pretty sure they like knowing I can't do anything to stop them. As a matter of fact, I'm a little shocked they didn't act on it right away. Maybe a part of their game is leaving me to drown in my own thoughts and fears.

I try to shift a little without waking either of them. I wish I was wearing more clothes. My shirt's already up around my waist, and I'm chilly but more afraid of what'll happen if either of them wakes up and sees me like this. They didn't put a blanket over me, or themselves for that matter. Of course, they are fully dressed, unlike me.

Even with a few inches between us, I can feel their body heat radiating from them, and part of me wants them to slide just a little closer. I force myself to stay still and not give in to the temptation their warmth is giving me, but after another while, I give up. I'm so fucking tired and cold. I just want to be able to go to sleep for a little while.

Carefully, I wiggle toward Mason, who is closest to me. My side presses against his arm, and I sigh as his body heat seeps into my cold skin. I try to stay still, but my body is greedy, and I move even closer, wanting more.

It doesn't take long for that to happen. Mason snorts in his sleep, then yawns. *Shit, I woke him up.* I watch him out of the corner of my eye, afraid to breathe. It's almost a shame he's so gorgeous.

His dark eyes find mine when he opens them, and a smile tugs at the corners of his mouth when he takes in the sight of me pressed up against him. "Cold?" he whispers, draping an arm around me.

"I'm fine," I whisper, terrified of his brother waking up. I try to pull away, but his arm is holding me in place like an iron bar.

"You look cold. There are goose bumps all up and down your legs. You're shaking, and your skin is cold to the touch."

"You didn't give me a blanket," I say softly, wondering if he is going to take this as backtalk and get angry.

"We're here to keep you warm." He smiles and runs his hand over my arm, sending a shiver down my body.

"I don't want this," I say in a tight voice. "I'd rather have a blanket or some clothes."

"I don't remember asking what you want."

Of course, he didn't. No one ever asks me what I want. It's like I don't even matter.

He runs a hand down and over my legs, chuckling when I try to move away from his touch. "Relax. I've never gotten a complaint from a woman."

Is that supposed to make me feel better?

A whimper works its way out of me when his hand moves up, skimming my skin before closing over my mound. At least I'm wearing panties, but it doesn't matter. He presses his fingers against my slit, his breath coming faster. Shorter. "This is nice and warm," he murmurs before nuzzling my neck. I squeeze my eyes shut and order myself not to react.

There's movement on my other side, and I know now I never had a chance. This was always going to happen. "Mm, what's this?" Evan rolls onto his side, facing me. "Having fun without waking me up? That's rude." Like this is a big joke.

Evan grins at his brother before sliding a hand under my shirt and fondling my breasts. I wish his warm hand wouldn't feel so good on my cold skin and that his touch didn't make my nipples go hard. "Hmm. You sure you don't want this? Your tits have other ideas." He raises the shirt over my chest, then up over my head until it's around my wrists. I've never been so humiliated, not even at work. Nothing Dimitri did was anything close to this.

Evan lowers his head, taking a nipple between his lips. I close my eyes and try to pretend I'm not here, but at the same time... it's doing something to me, the way he swirls his tongue in a slow circle before sucking. What starts off as a broken whimper turns into more of a moan when he sucks harder.

Mason runs his tongue over my throat before nipping my earlobe. "Enjoy yourself," he whispers, his breath hot and moist on my skin. "Don't hold back." His fingers move over my pussy, a thin strip of cotton in the way. When he presses harder, I want to ask for more even as I shake my head like I don't want it. *What's wrong with me?*

Evan releases my nipple and gets up. For a second, I want to believe that's as far as things will go—but when he starts unbuckling his belt, I know we're just getting started. The bulge jutting out in front of him makes my eyes go wide. "Like what you see?" He peels off his boxer briefs and reveals what has to be eight inches of thick, hard dick.

I pry my eyes away from it but can't stop staring at the rest of his body. Well-defined muscles, abs I could do laundry on. Thick thighs. All of it together is enough to stir up hunger deep in my core, and that only confuses me worse than ever.

Mason gets up to take his clothes off, too, while Evan crawls onto the foot of the bed. He reaches for my panties, and I try to fight him off. All it does is make him growl and take my ankles in his hands, squeezing until it almost hurts. "Stop fighting, we're not going to hurt you. We'll make you come before we fuck you."

"And after?" That's what I'm really worried about. I can handle sex. I can even handle it rough, but what I can't handle is being discarded after. "You're just going to keep me tied up as your sex slave?"

"It didn't have to be that way, but you showed us you can't be trusted," Mason answers.

Evan adds, "We saved your life. Consider this repayment."

It's not their words but rather the power in his hands that makes me stop fighting. He could hurt me. Badly.

"Good girl." It's a dark chuckle. I hate him for it. I hate him even more for pulling my panties off and spreading my thighs. Heat flushes my skin. Humiliation.

"You like this, don't you? Being helpless." Shaking my head, I try to tug on my restraints, but it does no good. He only chuckles as he parts my legs wider and stares down at my pussy. "Oh, yeah. You like it. Look how wet you are." He dips his fingers into that wetness, raising them so I can see how they glisten. My heart almost stops beating when he lifts them to his lips so he can lick them clean.

He grins at Mason. "You need to get a taste of this." But when Mason moves like he wants to take his brother's place, Evan shakes his head. "When I'm finished."

Before I know what's happening, he plunges down and licks at my slit. My hips jump up as I cry out in surprise and something else. Something so, so good.

Evan presses my hips to the mattress, holding me down with one arm draped over my belly. His tongue never stops moving, lapping up and down from my ass to my clit and back again. My nerves are on fire, sizzling hotter with every pass.

"Fuck, you're gorgeous." Mason strokes himself close to my face, watching his brother. "You like this?" he teases, strumming my nipple with his free hand. "Like being used like our slut? Like our little fuck doll?"

I open my mouth to say no, I don't like it, but he's too quick. He slides into my mouth, taking me by the back of the head when I try to turn my face away. He's just as long and thick as Evan, and I don't think I can take all of him.

"Don't even think about fighting. Suck this cock, doll." I have no choice but to take him in, to let him invade my mouth until he hits the back of my throat and makes me gag.

I can barely concentrate on Mason, not with Evan now spreading my lips with his fingers to expose my inner folds. He blows across them, and I shiver while Mason slides back before plunging in again. Evan's tongue sweeps over my clit, and I moan around Mason's cock without meaning to. It only makes them think I like it and want more when I don't. Or at least that's what I tell myself.

"Your mouth feels so fucking good." Mason buries himself in me until my nose is smashed against him, and I can't breathe. When I try to tell him I can't, he only grunts and drives himself in again. Again. So fast I can barely suck in air between thrusts while he holds my head still and fucks my face. I'm not a person to him. I'm a hole to fuck... a *doll*.

Something must be wrong with me because when I think that, the delicious sensations already running through me intensify until they're something I recognize. Pleasure. Strong enough to make me come, even. I don't want to. I hate this. I hate them.

But I love it, too. I want it. The idea of being their slut...

Evan's tongue flicks at my clit while two fingers work their way up into my tunnel. I moan, looking up at Mason, and the lust in his eyes almost sends me over the edge. Evan's fingers curve, and he presses against me from inside, and then I do lose it, clamping my legs tight around his head and shaking from the force of my orgasm. It rolls on and on through me, the sweetness stretching out until I don't think I can handle more. Am I broken? Is it ever going to stop?

It doesn't all at once. It happens slowly, easing up. Mason pulls out of my mouth, and I can finally breathe freely, sucking in huge gasps between whimpers as I recover from… whatever the hell just happened. I can't believe that happened.

"You're a squirter, huh?" Evan grins up at me, still between my legs, and now I feel the wetness he's talking about. It runs down my crack and soaks into the sheet.

"Out of my way." Mason just about pushes Evan off the bed so he can lick me clean. I don't know if I want to die of embarrassment or if I'm going to come again, watching him eagerly dive in and lick like he's starving for me.

"Fuck, you are perfect. Our perfect little doll." Evan watches my reaction, stroking himself. He's dripping onto his fist with excitement.

For me. They both want me. Oh, god, this is so hot.

Mason moves fast, getting on his knees, stroking himself before propping my thighs on his. The pressure from his head against my pussy makes me yelp in surprise and even fear. He's so big. They both are.

My reaction doesn't stop him. He plunges into me mercilessly, stretching and filling me up. My head falls back between my shoulders, the strain on my arms and wrists almost painful when he grips my hips and pulls me closer to him. "Too much!" I manage to gasp between thrusts, but he only pounds me harder.

"You can take it. I know you can. Take my fat cock and come while I fuck this tight cunt." His dirty words cause another zing of pleasure to course through my body.

Evan climbs up beside me, dripping precum on my chest. "Open your mouth, doll." He guides himself between my lips and sighs as he sinks deep, bottoming out with a satisfied groan.

"Tight…" Mason grunts. "So fucking tight."

"You like it when we stretch your tight little pussy?" Evan pulls my hair, and my eyes snap up to meet his. "Do you? I think you do, or else you wouldn't have come like you did. The good little girl likes to be dirty. Likes to be a slut fucked by two guys. You like getting your cunt pounded while choking on another cock."

No! No… Yes. Fuck! I think I'm going to come again. Why do I like it when he says things like that in his deep, dirty voice? It makes everything more intense, hotter. My insides pulse with every deep thrust into my mouth and pussy, and I can only imagine how filthy this looks. Two men using my sweaty, tied-up body. The image makes me moan.

"You wanna come on my brother's cock before you come on mine, doll?" Evan's balls slap against my cheek with every thrust as he continues muttering dirty things to me.

"Get yourself nice and wet again so I can fuck you deep?" I nod slightly, ashamed and hotter than ever.

And close. So close. I would tell Mason, but I think he knows when my muscles start clenching around him. "Come for me," he urges through gritted teeth, fucking me faster. Harder. Until I do what he asks, my insides tighten around him and hold him still before melting into sweet spasms that spread through my core and make me sob out my release.

Evan pulls back, leaving saliva dripping down my chin. He moves down my body as Mason pulls out. Taking my hips in his hands, Evan pulls me around until my ass is almost hanging off the side of the bed. Like the doll they think I am, I let him position me. My limbs are too tired to fight, and my arms are still tied to the headboard, the fabric sliding with the movement.

I'm about to ask them to untie me when I feel another cock at my entrance. My words get caught in my throat when he pushes inside me so deep, I can feel him in my belly.

Mason took me hard, but Evan? He punishes me, slamming like a jackhammer until I understand what it means when something hurts so good. His rhythm has me dancing on the line between pain and pleasure, grinding my teeth against the screams threatening to tear their way out of me.

Mason stares at my tits, transfixed by the way they bounce every time Evan crashes into me. His fist is a blur, moving up and down over his cock in time with Evan's merciless thrusts. I don't know whether I'm going to come again or pass out. Maybe both.

Evan adds a thumb to his onslaught, circling my clit. My head bobs up and down in approval before I know what's happening. I should hate this. I should hate them. But all I want now is for this to never stop.

But it does, ending with me throwing my head back and howling. Evan pulls out fast, and for a second, it's just my cries and their heavy breathing. I open my eyes in time to see the first spurts of cum splashing across my stomach, my tits, and my thighs as both of them come at once.

I've never felt so used. But I've also never felt so satisfied. Only when the fog of my orgasmic high clears do I want to cry. This is it, the part where they discard me, leave me tied to the bed, and go somewhere else. Or maybe just lock me up in a basement. Either way, I'll be alone like always. Used, discarded, and left behind.

I close my eyes and pretend to be somewhere else. Pretend that someone actually cares about me enough not to leave me.

Turning my face away, I keep my eyes closed as the guys move off the bed. I hear the door open and them moving around. I hold in my tears, wanting them to leave before I let myself sob into the pillow.

Instead of them leaving, I feel one of them moving closer. I flinch when I feel something warm between my legs. My eyes fly open and connect with Evan's smug face.

I watch him in shock as he gently and deliberately cleans me up with a warm washcloth.

"Don't worry, we take care of what's ours." He smiles and finishes cleaning me up. The warm rag slides over my sensitive skin, and he is actually careful not to hurt me as he cleans my sore pussy.

When he is satisfied with his work, he drops the washcloth next to the bed and moves me back into the center.

Mason appears at the other side of us, holding a thick comforter in his arms. "If you behave tomorrow, we'll talk about leaving you untied, but right now, it's safest for all of us to keep you like this."

I simply nod, knowing that arguing won't get me anywhere.

"Can I get some water?" I ask, looking at the bottle sitting on the nightstand.

"Sure." Evan grabs the bottle and unscrews the cap while Mason covers me with the blanket.

Sliding his hand under my head, Evan lifts it slightly while holding the bottle to my lips. I take a few greedy gulps before shaking my head, signaling that I am done. He puts the water where it stood before and climbs back onto the bed.

Both guys spread out next to me, tucking the blanket up to my chin.

"Comfortable?" Mason asks, and all I can do is nod.

Even with my hands tied, I've never felt so taken care of.

They didn't leave me. Even after they got what they wanted, they cared for me instead of leaving. How are my kidnappers better to me than my family ever was?

That's the last thing on my mind before exhaustion finally makes me pass out.

MASON

One thing about Evan and me: we learn our lesson the first time. You don't grow up how and where we did without learning to avoid mistakes. No room for fucking off. No lapses in judgment.

Which is why I watch as Frankie uses the bathroom the morning after our three-way. "Do you need to be here for this?" She hangs her head in humiliation.

"Yeah, because otherwise, you might try to take a header out the window." I fold my arms, leaning against the wall near the door. Truthfully, I've never cared much for watching a woman piss, but this is how it has to be.

"I won't do that again."

"So you say." Once she's finished, I haul her out of the room by one arm and lead her downstairs to the kitchen.

Evan's throwing a quick breakfast together. Cereal and coffee. Our go-to since neither of us knows much about cooking.

"Do you live here together?" It's the first question she's asked that doesn't have to do with herself or what brought us to her. I nod before pulling out a chair and guiding her to it. "Just the two of you in this big house?"

"What about it?"

She shrugs, cheeks darkening. "I don't know. I was just wondering. My whole apartment could fit in this kitchen." Her eyes are wide as she curiously looks around. I have to bite back an explanation while wondering why I want to explain myself at all. She doesn't need to know how we grew up, how when we were kids, we promised each other that we'd never be without plenty of space when we were adults.

Evan slides a bowl of cereal in front of her. "Eat," he grunts. She grabs the spoon he'd already laid out and starts eating with her head down while the two of us drink our coffee. Neither of us needs to say it out loud, but I know we're both thinking it. We need to figure out why we were sent to her and who we're up against.

As usual, Evan plunges in the second she's finished. He pushes the bowl away from her, and his sudden change of demeanor makes her sit up straighter. "Who did you piss off enough to want you dead?"

She flinches and looks away, and I know we're on the same page. She can pretend all she wants to be innocent and sweet or whatever, but she wouldn't have ended up on a hit list if she didn't make the wrong move against the wrong person.

And as we learned overnight, she's not innocent. Not even a little bit.

Evan doesn't have my patience. "Well? Start talking." He shoves her chair a little like that'll jumpstart her memory. All it does is make her flinch.

"Calm down, Evan," I say in warning. "All you're doing is scaring her more. She is gonna tell us, aren't you, doll?"

She hangs her head even more, hair falling down like a waterfall on either side of her face. "I thought about it all night, and there's only one person I can think of, but it still doesn't make any sense. I mean, I knew he was an asshole, but why would he put a hit on me for something so stupid and small?"

"So you crossed somebody." I pull up another chair, turning it around and straddling it. Folding my arms over the back, I sigh. "What was it? Did you get a little greedy? Dip into the safe when you thought nobody was paying attention? Somebody's always watching, sweetheart."

I can't believe how disappointed I am that she would do something that stupid. It's one thing to work for a criminal—we all have to make money and survive. It was obvious this girl lived alone. Even a shithole apartment requires rent payments.

But to cross somebody like that? It takes a special kind of stupidity.

Her head snaps up, eyes narrowed and blazing. "No. I didn't steal anything. I've never stolen a thing in my life, so go to hell with that bullshit."

"You sure about that?" Evan smirks at me from behind her.

"I'm sure. I earn what I make. I don't steal it." She tosses her head back, proud all of a sudden. "I don't steal people, either. But I guess since you do, you can't imagine being honest."

"I'm honestly sick of your holier-than-thou bullshit," Evan growls. "Just get to it. What did you do?"

Her shoulders sink a little, and some of the fire leaves her eyes. I place my hand on her shoulder and rub calming circles on her skin using my thumb. "Tell us."

"The only thing I can think of is the fight I had with my boss two nights ago. My ex-boss, I guess. I sort of figured I'd lost my job."

I exchange another look with my brother because her story is not adding up. Nobody puts a twenty-thousand-dollar hit on an employee because they had an argument. "What started the fight?"

She looks at the floor again, and before her hair covers her face, I catch sight of the way her cheeks flush. "He wanted me to do things I wouldn't do. I told him I never would, no matter what he offered. But he kept trying."

Instinct makes the hair on the back of my neck stand up. Now we're getting somewhere.

"What did he want?" Evan asks, walking around the chair and coming to a stop next to me. He's just as curious now as I am.

"It's disgusting. I don't even want to say."

"You'd better tell us," I warn. "Remember, we're trying to help you." All she does is snicker.

"Enough of this." Evan goes to her, reaching out to take a handful of her hair. He yanks it back, and she gasps. "Talk. Now."

"He wanted me to sleep with one of his customers." Her eyes are wide and pained. "Before that, he spent the whole time I worked at his club trying to convince me to take my clothes off. I was only a waitress, but he wanted me to be a stripper."

"I can see why." I look her up and down, imagining her onstage. "A body like yours? With those tits and that ass? You could make a fortune."

"I don't want to make money that way. Don't I get to say what I want to do with my own body?" She catches her bottom lip under her teeth, and I know she's thinking about earlier this morning. About what we've done to that body of hers. She didn't have a say in that even though it was obvious she liked it.

Evan lets go of her hair, grunting. "Fine. He wanted you to strip, and you kept saying no. Then he, what, approached you about fucking one of his customers?"

"Approached?" She snorts, rolling her eyes. "You're making it sound a lot nicer than it was. He cornered me and told me I had to have sex with a customer or else I'd lose my job."

"Did he at least offer you a lot of cash for it?" I ask. She shoots me a filthy look that shouldn't make my cock stir, but it does. "It's an honest question."

"Yes. He offered money for it. The customer wanted to pay twenty-five thousand. I'd get ten."

"Wow. Not bad for a night's work."

"Screw you," she snarls at me. So that was all it took to get her to stop sniveling and trembling. "I'm not a whore. I'll wait on customers at a sleazy strip joint, but I'm not having sex for money."

"Okay, okay, fine. You're too good for sex work." Evan shrugs. "So for that, he wants you dead?"

She bites her lip again. "I hit him. That might have something to do with it."

Oh. That changes things.

"He had me cornered in his office, backed up against his desk. He was leaning over me." She gags a little. "His cologne was choking me, his breath was sour, and he was in my face, you know? Telling me I was going to have sex with this guy because it would mean a lot of money for him, and this was a guy who already spends a lot of money at the club. He's there all the time. So I guess Dimitri didn't want to lose that, either."

"Wait. Dimitri?" Evan's a little gentler this time, tipping her head back with a finger under her chin instead of a handful of hair. "That's his name?"

"Yes. Dimitri Sokoloff."

Fuck me. I don't need to look at Evan to know we're on the same page. "Shit. If we knew his name before now, we wouldn't have needed to ask."

She shrinks back a little. "It was a job. I needed the money. I didn't have to like him."

I can't help but bristle when I think of Frankie being ogled in a place like that. The way the men there must've drooled over her body and her face. All the times they must've propositioned her. All the times she must've been groped and fondled and—

And he let it happen. He encouraged it.

I shoot up from the chair when it's all too much to think about while sitting still. There's something dark and murderous inside me, and now all I want is to walk into Dimitri's club and gun down every single fucking customer there.

While he watches. While he knows the entire time that I'm coming for him once I've gotten everybody else out of the way. I want him to dread the final moment of his life, knowing it's all about to come to an end. Nothing short of that will satisfy the hunger deep in my core.

"How did it end?" Evan's teeth are clenched so tight I can barely make out what he's saying. He's feeling it, too. The need for vengeance. She is ours, and we're the only ones who get to touch her.

"I slid past him somehow. I don't even remember. I was so desperate, and it happened so fast. I was…" She lets out a little sniffle. "I was afraid he'd try to rape me. Or at least beat me. He was so, so angry, and I was sure he'd hurt me. So I picked up the first thing I touched. A chair."

"A chair?" My jaw drops.

"It wasn't a big, heavy chair. Just a wooden one." Like that makes it better or less surprising. "He laughed right up until I swung it. I don't think he thought I'd go through with it."

"You hit him with a chair?" Evan sounds like he's choking on something.

Her head bobs up and down. "I had to. I had to stop him. He fell on his knees, but I couldn't have hurt him all that bad. I dropped the chair and ran out of there. I didn't even get my last paycheck."

A small thing to worry about, but then I guess that's easy for me to say. One thought back to the shitty little apartment we took her from, and I know she had to be living hand to mouth. She must've been damn scared if she was willing to run out of there like the place was on fire.

"And that's it?" I prompt. "You didn't see him after that?"

"No. He was screaming at me when I ran out, but I haven't seen him since. I never talked to anybody else from the club, like the girls who worked there. Nobody." She looks back and forth between us. "Why?"

Why? Because this seems like a petty, childish reason to put a hit out on somebody. All because she told him she wouldn't fuck a customer for money. Because she wouldn't take her clothes off. Because she stood up to him and even hit him with a chair— as small as she is, I doubt it hurt him. Falling to his knees because a girl swung a chair at him. What a fucking pussy.

Enough of a fucking pussy to want her out of the way, permanently, over something as stupid as this. She hurt his pride, that's all. Fragile asshole.

We have a lot to discuss, none of which we can talk about in front of her. I take her by the arm and haul her to her feet. "Come on. Back to bed."

"What? Can't I—?"

"No. You can't." I don't care what she was about to ask. It doesn't matter. We're harboring a girl with a price on her head, a price set by one of the most notorious assholes in town. Everybody knows the rumors of the girls who disappeared while working at his clubs. Looks like they're more than rumors.

"Please don't leave me here," she begs as I tie her to the headboard in my room, and it almost makes me stop. I don't particularly want to leave her; I'd rather slide into my bed with her and forget about everything. But I can't.

"We'll be downstairs. You can yell if you need something."

She looks away, clearly unhappy with my answer. Right now, this is the safest place for her.

Grinding my molars, I force myself to leave and ignore her soft sniffles.

She's the least of our problems right now. And whether she knows it or not, we're the least of hers.

FRANKIE

I think the worst part is not knowing what's going on in the house. I can hear them talking and moving stuff around downstairs, but I have no idea what they're up to.

At least it's a comfortable bed, but I'm still tied up. I can't exactly bring myself to be grateful.

Right now, I can't even be grateful I'm alive. Is that wrong? But who could blame me? I have no say in anything; I can't even pee in private. And I'm basically their sex slave—unless the stuff that happened overnight was a mistake or a one-off sort of thing.

Something tells me it wasn't. If there's one thing I've learned, it's that nothing comes for free. They could've killed me, but instead, they brought me here. So now I owe them. Yet, I still don't know what they're doing. What they have in mind other than sex.

Why did they accept a hit job in the first place? Is that what they do for a living? I'm in the home of two hitmen who, what? Grew a conscience at the last minute?

What if they decide I'm not worth the trouble? What if they kill me anyway? I'm not sure whether that would be a good or a bad thing. Because if this is the rest of my life, I don't want any part of it. I can't imagine being tied up all day just to be used at night.

Tears start forming in my eyes, and the only thing keeping them at bay is remembering how they treated me after they fucked me last night. They cleaned me up and tucked me in, making sure I was somewhat comfortable as they slept beside me. Something about being sandwiched between them was comforting, like nothing could get to me. I know it's probably something my mind makes up. They only took me for selfish reasons, not because they would actually protect me.

Hours have passed since breakfast. I have no idea how many. There isn't much of anything besides furniture, nothing personal, nothing to tell me anything about who Mason is. Evan's room was the same, come to think of it. I might as well be in a furniture store, tied up to a display bed. Yet the house is so big, so nice, the appliances in the kitchen shining and new. But it doesn't look like they're ever used.

Who are these guys?

I'm so bored, so desperate for anything to take my mind off what's happened to me that even these two seem interesting and worth getting to know. I guess if I'm going to be here for a while, I might as well.

It's sleep I need more than anything, though, considering I spent most of the morning thinking and dreading instead of sleeping. I'm struggling not to cry because I can't use my hands to wipe away my tears or blow my stuffy nose.

I must doze off at some point because I wake with a start when the bedroom door opens.

Evan marches in, scowling the way he always does. "I made you a sandwich." He leaves a paper plate on the bed with what looks and smells like tuna salad on white bread. "I figured you would be hungry."

"Is it lunchtime?"

He looks around, still scowling. "Right. No clock. Yeah, it's past one." When I wiggle my hands around, he takes the hint and unties me. I have to shake my hands out to get the blood flowing again before picking up one half of the sandwich.

"So, what have you been doing today?" I ask before taking a bite.

To my surprise, he laughs. When all I do is look at him, chewing, he laughs again. "Are you honestly asking?"

"Yeah. I hear you guys moving around a lot downstairs. I can hear you talking, but I can't hear what you're saying. It sounds like you've been busy, and I'm… ahm, bored."

"Yeah, we're busy." He ignores my last statement, and I can practically see a wall coming down between us. So he's not going to share anything.

I take a different route. "Today is Christmas Eve, isn't it?"

"All day long."

My throat tightens as pain blooms in my chest. I do my best to push them both back while eating, keeping my eyes down so he can't see the tears that sprang into them all of a sudden. "I have to admit, this isn't where I figured I would be spending it."

He snickers like it's funny. "What were your plans?"

"I didn't really have any."

"No family or anything like that?" There's interest in his voice, and it occurs to me that he would need to know.

After all, there might be somebody looking for me. Somebody who isn't Dimitri.

But there isn't. "No. I've been on my own for a few years now."

"Friends?"

"Not really. I was never any good at making friends… or keeping them. Maybe a couple of girls at the club, but we were more acquaintances than anything. I'm too awkward." I can't believe I just admitted that. Then again, the man has seen more of me than any man ever did before him, so why bother keeping anything to myself?

Silence spreads between us as I finish one half of the sandwich. It was nothing fancy, but I didn't realize how hungry I was until I started eating. It doesn't even bother me that he's sitting on the edge of the bed, watching me like I'm an animal in a zoo. Maybe he wouldn't if I hadn't tried to get out last night, but I couldn't help it. I had to try something. Now I wish I hadn't because, of course, I would've frozen to death before I got anywhere. I was too panicked to think straight.

Finally, he asks, "What were you going to do today if you didn't have family or friends to spend it with?"

"I was going to watch TV. Christmas shows, movies, whatever I could find. I was planning on getting some

Chinese from a place a few blocks away. It's what I usually do on Christmas Eve."

He snorts, and I look up at him, ready to be pissed that he's making fun of me. Except he isn't. His forehead is creased, his brows drawing together. "That's depressing."

"Not compared to this." He almost cracks a smile, but not quite. Like there's a real person in there, somewhere.

Don't do that. Don't make him human.

Once I'm finished, he takes the plate and leaves it on the nightstand. "You need to get cleaned up. I'll draw you a bath. Come on." He doesn't open the matter up for discussion. Standing, he unties me and waits for me to join him. I do without thinking because what's the alternative? I might make mistakes, but I try not to make the same ones twice.

And if the way they're treating me right now is the result of my trying to get away, I don't even want to think about how much worse it could get if I make another attempt. That's why I sit on the closed toilet lid and watch as Evan turns the taps in the tub. He pulls out a couple of towels and leaves them for me, then turns my way with an expectant look on his face.

Oh. Right. He's not going to leave me alone.

I can't help but shiver a little as I turn away, taking the hem of my shirt in my hands. "No."

"What?" I look at him over my shoulder.

"Don't turn away from me." There's something different in his eyes now. Something I recognize. I've seen that look more times than I can remember, only I've never been in this position—defenseless.

That's why I turn slowly back around, forcing myself not to look away or be embarrassed. *I didn't ask for any of this. None of this is my fault. I have nothing to be ashamed of.* Thinking this makes it easier for me to take the shirt off.

That, and the heat between my legs when our eyes meet. I can't help but remember what he and Mason did to me, how they made me feel. Is it going to happen again? I should want nothing less, but that's not the truth of what's going on in my head or elsewhere while I slide out of my panties.

He looks me up and down, breathing hard. "In the tub."

I do as I'm told because I know better, and the warm water is such a pleasure. I sink into it, only now realizing how sore my muscles are from being in the same position for hours.

When Evan kneels next to the tub, I can't help but go stiff. He ignores my reaction in favor of soaping up a washcloth. Without asking, he pushes aside the hair hanging down my back and starts washing my neck, my shoulders, and across my collarbone. He's not exactly rough, but he's not gentle, either.

"You know, we did this for you. Bringing you here was to save your life." I'm not looking at him, choosing to stare at the wall in front of me instead, but I hear the hesitation in his voice. He takes his time, the words coming out like a series of grunts. Like he's not used to talking this way to anybody. "It's not like we decided to keep you for ourselves if that's what you think."

His words sink in, and I know he's telling the truth. I feel it. "I guess I should thank you."

"You're right. You should." He washes my arm, and a brief glimpse of his profile tells me he's grinning. He's actually capable of humor.

Suddenly, something else occurs to me. "What about you? Did you two have any plans for Christmas Eve?"

He snickers, sarcastic again. "Did you notice any decorations around the house? We don't exactly celebrate around here."

"I'm sorry."

The motion from the washcloth slows almost to a stop. "Why?"

Now I wish I hadn't said it. But I can't take it back, either. "I don't know. I guess it just makes me feel sorry for you two. Do you at least get each other gifts?"

"Do we strike you as those types of people?" I see his point. Then he sighs, continuing to wash my other arm this time. "We visit our mother. We do the whole Christmas thing with her because it makes her happy."

That's the last thing I expected to hear. "Wow."

"That so surprising?" He moves on to my legs, lifting one into the air and starting at my feet. "Of course, we have a mother. We weren't just, like, hatched."

"It's nice that you get a chance to celebrate, anyway." I bite my lip, staring at the wall, trying to disassociate from the situation. Not that there's anything terribly wrong about this—in fact, being taken care of is sort of nice. Even if it's a little strange. Even if I can't stop expecting his touch to change, to become more intimate.

Even if I want it to.

At least he gets to celebrate the holiday. What will they do to me? Leave me tied up here, all alone on Christmas Day?

None of this is my fault, but I'm the one who gets to suffer for it.

When the washcloth brushes over my breasts, everything else goes out the window. Heat blooms fresh in my core, making my pussy tingle with each brush over my nipples. He's not washing anymore. He's massaging, his eyes fixed on my body. He strums a thumb over my nipple, and I bite back a moan. This shouldn't turn me on like it does. Everything about this is wrong.

But how does he know just what to do? The slightest touch and everything I thought I knew blows away. Instead of closing my legs when his hand slides over my belly, heading south, I open them. I invite him. It's so wrong, all of it, but nothing could stop me. Not when I know what happens when he touches me like this.

"When I think of what might've happened to you last night if it had been anybody but us…" He strokes my outer lips, his breathing picking up speed. "That I might never have gotten to touch this body…"

I close my eyes, my head falling back, but the sharpness in his voice snaps me out of it. "Look at me. Look in my eyes." I do as he says, staring into the dark depths, afraid of what I might find but more afraid of him stopping. That's the last thing I want. If only he would never stop. When he dips into my seam, spreading my lips and touching the part of me that's hot and aching, I gasp, and he chuckles. "That's right. Look at me. Let me watch you."

I have no idea what's going on. What kind of game is this? Am I losing? Do I even care? He works my clit, stroking it in tight little circles, and nothing matters as much as the tension that has me lifting my hips, silently begging for more.

"Nobody else has ever made you come the way we did. Right?"

I can only shake my head, whimpering when he increases the pressure, making fireworks explode in my head while my hips roll in slow circles. I'm breathing heavily, and so is he, our eyes locked. He's so close. Almost close enough to kiss.

He groans softly, staring at my mouth like he knows what I'm thinking. His eyes meet mine again. "Come for me now. Let me see you. Let me hear you. Don't hold back, doll." When my eyes threaten to slide shut again—I can't help it—he uses his other hand to take a fistful of my hair. One little jerk is enough to open my eyes again.

It's happening. I welcome it, want it, work for it. My hips jerk up and down until water splashes both of us. "Oh... Oh, my god..."

"Let go." He pulls my hair a little harder, and for some reason, the heat intensifies, my hips jerking faster. So close...

The sweetest explosion starts low in my belly and radiates outward, all through the rest of my body. Wave after wave of bliss. I let out a choked sob, my hands gripping the sides of the tub, my body trembling from the force.

Evan smiles. The first genuine smile I've seen so far. "Good girl."

Before I know what's happening, something catches in my chest. A twinge of pain, sadness—all of my emotions are so much stronger and more vivid in these first moments after coming so hard. It's like a dam is breaking, and all of a sudden, everything wants to pour out.

Which is why I start crying. I can't help it any more than I could help what Evan just made me do. It comes out in huge sobs. I feel like my heart is breaking.

And he's still here, hovering over me now. Is he concerned or just freaked out? "What's the matter?"

I almost don't want to say. At first, I shake my head, ready to lie and say it's nothing, but that only makes me cry harder. "Why did you let me live? What was the point?"

"What?" He stands, pissed off now. I can see it in the way his jaw tightens and the way his eyes narrow. I'm not crying hard enough to miss it, and I wish I was.

"Why didn't you just kill me?" When all he does is stare at me, I pull my knees up to my chest and touch my forehead to them, trembling. "What's the point of me being alive? No one is gonna miss me anyway." I know I'm throwing myself a pity party, but I also feel like I have every right to. I didn't pity myself when I spent the last three Christmases alone, and I wasn't planning on doing so this year, not until I was almost killed and then kidnapped.

For a while, the only sounds in the room are my sniffling and his breathing. At this point, I don't care anymore if he's angry or if he wants to hurt me or kill me. The thought of spending Christmas tied to a bed, all alone, is too much to handle. I might as well be dead if this is what the rest of my life will look like: a prisoner in their home, theirs to do whatever they want with. It doesn't matter that my body likes it. My heart never will.

He finally picks up a towel, holding it in front of me. "Get dried off. I'll wait outside in the hall. Don't get any ideas." Any warmth I heard in his voice earlier is gone now, but still, he is giving me a moment of privacy.

Baby steps.

MASON

"*T*his is a stupid fucking idea." Evan shakes his head, stepping back to take in everything I put together. We sort of worked together, but only up to a point. After lunch, he went to a dark place, and I knew better than to get on his case about it. I know that place, too. I've been there plenty of times.

"I don't think it's stupid. I think it's brilliant… if it works." I get up from where I've been kneeling and shrug. "How many years has Mom been bugging us to bring a girl home? Just imagine how happy she'll be if we bring Frankie."

"All I'm imagining is Frankie running to the police at the first chance she gets."

"She won't," I quip, not even sure why. I have no evidence of it, but something tells me she wouldn't rat us out. "If we want her to play along, we're going to have to make her happy. At least for tonight."

"I still vote for leaving her here. Taking her anywhere is too much of a risk."

We've been through this at least ten times since breakfast. "And what if she gets out? We can't leave her alone. Besides." I lower my brow, shooting him a look. "What if there's a problem? What if there's a fire or something?"

"Stop making up shit." He snickers, shaking his head. "What would be the chances of a random fire?"

I have to turn away from him because if I don't, I might knock him flat. I can't stand it when he's in this mood any more than he can when the roles are reversed. Instead of bickering, I admire my work. Considering I only had a few hours to put everything together, I don't think it turned out half bad. Especially since this is the first tree I've decorated in years. We didn't even have ornaments or lights, and it's not easy to find them on Christmas Eve.

I managed. There isn't an overworked clerk who won't check the stockroom if you flash the right amount of cash.

I even went so far as to bring home some prepared foods for dinner, all of which are warming in the oven. I don't know if Frankie likes turkey and all that shit, but hopefully, she'll appreciate the effort. It's enough to make me grit my teeth, bending over backward like this, but Mom is worth it. Nothing's more important than keeping her happy.

"Okay. I'll go up and get her." I can't believe how much this matters. Of all the times of the year to have a situation like this. There are only a few days we absolutely can't go without visiting Mom, and tomorrow's one of them. Either we threaten Frankie into behaving—which could make her worse and cause her to run for help the second we get to the house—or we ease her into it with a little goodwill and some glittery ornaments. I'll never get the fucking glitter off my skin now. She'd better appreciate this.

I find her lying on her side, hands clasped in front of her face, wrists still bound. I left the light on the last time I checked on her so she wouldn't be stuck in the dark, but it occurs to me now that there's more I could do to make her comfortable than turning on a light and giving her clean sweats to wear. "Hey. We'll have dinner soon. And there's something else for you down there."

She brings to mind a wary animal when she lifts her head, eyes narrowed. "What is it?"

"You'll have to come down and see." For fuck's sake, this is stupid. *Think of Mom. This is for her.* I force as pleasant an expression as possible before going to the bed and untying the knots so she's free to get up. "You look cute in my clothes, by the way." Better than cute. Frankie's one of those women who looks even hotter wearing oversized clothes, a little rumpled and sloppy.

She ignores the comment, following me into the hall and down the stairs. Her footsteps slow once she catches sight of the lights gleaming off the living room floor. "Oh…" She stops, peering into the room, holding the banister like she might fall over if she lets go.

The tree did turn out well. I've always been a more-the-merrier sort of person, so I put on as many lights as the thing could hold. She likes lights. That much, I already knew. "We thought you might like a little bit of holiday stuff tonight."

She turns to me, beaming, eyes shining. Holy shit. It's like she punched me in the gut. All it took was a little shopping and decorating to make her glow the way she is. "It's beautiful! This is what you were so busy with today?"

"And other things." Some of which she doesn't need to know about. "Come on. Dinner should be warmed up by now. I'm starving."

"I guess so, after doing all that." Her gaze falls on the wrapped gifts under the tree, brows lifting when she looks my way again.

"No. I didn't do the wrapping. I have my limits." I can't believe how much lighter I feel as I lead her to the kitchen, where Evan is fumbling his way through taking things out of the oven. If our mother could see us now, practically doing headstands to appease this girl, she'd laugh herself into a fit, then scream in joy and hug us until we couldn't breathe.

"It smells incredible." She's so shy, so tentative, but so happy.

"I hope you're hungry. I bought a lot of food." There are eight containers lined up on the counter. "Do you like traditional holiday stuff?"

"I love it. I can't remember the last time I had…" She shakes her head a little. "I love it."

So far, so good. I try to catch Evan's eye, but he's deliberately avoiding me in favor of plating turkey, stuffing, and potatoes. I hand Frankie a plate, so she can fix her own food, trying not to grin at the way her eyes widen when she takes in everything I brought home.

Nobody ever told me what making somebody happy feels like. It seems unfair that she's this excited over so little.

She couldn't have had much else going on in her life before we stepped into it. I know what it's like to have nothing and for the littlest things to mean more than they should.

"This is so great." She beams at me before plopping potatoes on her plate.

"There's more coming after this."

"Check out Santa," Evan mumbles. I don't think she heard him. I decide to pretend I didn't—otherwise, we'll end up fighting and blowing the whole scheme to hell.

We sit down and basically gorge ourselves. The girl's got an appetite, but then again, she hasn't eaten much today and probably didn't before then. She's so thin. I can't believe how much I want to take care of her. No wonder I faltered when it came time to kill her.

Once we're finished eating, I lead her to the living room. "There are a few things for you under the tree." If she's suspicious, she doesn't show it.

Though she does raise an eyebrow. "Why did you buy me gifts?"

"It felt right." She'll understand. She'll have to. I stand back, Evan behind me, and watch as she tears into the first package with her name written on the label.

She gasps, lifting the jacket from the box. "I hope it fits okay." How fucking lame do I sound?

"I'm sure it will." Her eyes bulge. "This had to be expensive."

"Don't worry about that." Yes, it was, but that's kind of the point. "Keep going."

She opens a pair of jeans, a sweater, and leather boots. "I bought a couple of different sizes," I admit when she holds them up. "I can always return the ones that don't fit."

"I don't know what to say." She lowers the boots, and now there's obvious suspicion in her eyes when they meet mine. "Other than to ask what this is all about. You bought me an entire outfit." She nudges a slim box next. "I bet there's underwear in here."

Evan chuckles. "Told you she'd see through it."

When her face falls, I want to murder him. The pain in the ass couldn't be bothered to play along even for a little while.

"See through what?" Frankie asks in a much smaller voice than before. All the light, all the happiness. It's gone.

Evan blurts it out before I can find the words. "We're visiting our mom tomorrow, and you have to come with us. You and Mason will have to pretend to be a couple, so Mom doesn't get the wrong idea."

She blinks rapidly. "The wrong idea? You mean the right idea. You don't want her to know the truth." Her gaze swings my way, and I can't believe how much I want to shrivel under it. "This was all your way of buttering me up, so I'd agree to go along."

"You don't have to go along." Evan takes a slow step toward her, then another. "We can leave you here tied to the bed all day… or even better, we can take you back to your apartment and do what should've been done last night." I understand why he said it, even if I know he doesn't mean it. Or does he? She's obviously done something to piss him off.

"Listen." I hold up a hand to stop him from scaring her worse than she already is. If there wasn't so much hanging in the balance, I might feel differently. "We did you a favor last night by sparing your life. I don't think you understand the risk we took. If Dimitri catches even a hint of you being alive, he'll track us down."

"Not to ask if we wanna go out for a holiday drink, either," Evan adds in a low voice.

"The least you can do is play along tomorrow," I finish. "End of story."

Her gaze drifts down to the gifts, the crumpled paper. "Got it. You didn't have to go through all this trouble. I'll do whatever you need."

Hearing her sound that defeated wouldn't sting the way it does if I hadn't already heard her sounding so happy.

Merry Christmas to me.

At least nobody tried to have sex with me last night. Thankfully, because my pussy is still sore. Every step I took yesterday, I could feel how they fucked me the other night. I still slept between them, this time with my ankle tied to the footboard instead of my wrists. I pointed out how uncomfortable it is to sleep that way, and Mason didn't put up an argument. I think he feels shitty after last night.

Which he should. Bribing me like that. For a second, I thought he cared. I thought maybe Evan told him how sad I was, and they were making it up to me.

Stupid. So stupid. They don't care about me, just their own needs.

But Mason made a point, too. They didn't have to let me live. And if Dimitri ever found out... yeah, we'll all be screwed. They had to know that since I doubt I was their first assignment. Not if they can afford such a nice house, not to mention the gifts Mason picked up.

Like the leather jacket I shrug into before leaving the house. It's as soft as butter, just like the knee-high boots I'm wearing. He picked up three pairs, and the smallest are the ones that fit. The red sweater is actually one-hundred-percent cashmere. I can't even imagine how much money all this cost.

"Ready?" Evan looks me up and down and gives me a single nod. "You look good. She'll love you." He then hands me a stack of festively wrapped packages for her. He and Mason are holding bags and boxes, too. They must really spoil her.

This is going to be interesting.

"Remember what we talked about." Mason loads his packages into a car way nicer than the one they used last night. He then takes the ones I'm holding and closes the BMW's trunk. "We've been dating six months now. We met at work. You're an assistant."

"At an investment agency." What a joke. They kill people for a living, but she thinks they're investment guys.

"Right." He strokes his freshly shaved jaw. I almost like him more when he's scruffy, but both brothers have cleaned up big time for today. I wish they weren't so hot. I wish I didn't want to lick their abs and other parts whenever I get a whiff of the cologne they wear. Two different brands, but both are musky and spicy and capable of making me want to forget how they kidnapped me.

Mason drives with me in the front seat. Neither of them trusts me, even with the doors locked. All I can do is look out the window as we roll down the road, noticing how many homes are fully decked out today. One house has a driveway practically overflowing with cars. People greet each other, hugging and generally being happy.

I wish I was one of them. Any of them. I have to fight the tears threatening to well up in my eyes. Wouldn't want to upset Mom.

"This is the place?" I ask when we pull into what looks more like a luxury hotel than a nursing home.

"What? You think we'd put our mother in some shithole?" Evan sounds like he's insulted.

"No, it's just I never saw a nursing home this nice. You don't visualize someplace like this when you think about a home." The sprawling yard is sparkling with lights in all the trees and bushes and a huge nativity scene out front.

Fresh wreaths decorated with big, sparkly bows hang on most of the windows.

"She deserves it," he informs me in a tight voice. I'm starting to get the idea he'd kill anybody who looked at his mom the wrong way. It's almost endearing.

Not as endearing as the reaction we receive upon entering a room a few doors down from the big, sunny lobby. She's sitting in a rocking chair by the window, wearing a red velvet dress and a sprig of holly tucked in her gray hair. "My boys are here to see me!" Her voice is weak but sweet and full of love.

She adores them. Her sons are hitmen, and she adores them.

We leave the presents in front of a cute little tree in the corner. "Merry Christmas, Mom." Evan leans over and gives her a hug. Her smile is almost painfully joyful. The same happens when Mason hugs her. She kisses his cheek before patting it.

"My handsome boys. Better looking every time I see the two of you." Then she notices me—except for a second, where she looks confused, her smile never moves. "And who is this?"

Mason slides an arm around my waist. "Mom, this is Frankie." He's holding me almost tight enough to hurt, but

I manage to smile. Not for their sake. For hers.

"Mrs. Pavlis, it's so nice to meet you. I hope you don't mind me being here on Christmas."

She reaches for my hand and takes it in both of hers. They're small, the way she is, but there's strength in them. "Sweetheart, you're the first girl either of my sons has ever introduced to me. That makes you special."

She has no idea.

Evan clears his throat. "That's not true. Remember Becca from high school?"

"Her." She rolls her eyes, and I see where Evan gets his attitude from. "She doesn't count, that little floozy." Mason chokes on his laughter, and I can't help but giggle when Evan's face goes red.

She then eyes all the presents. "You know you don't need to go to all this trouble." Though it's obvious she enjoys it. What she enjoys more is when her sons pull up chairs and sit close to her while she opens them.

At first, I thought coming here today was a joke. That Evan and Mason couldn't have the hearts to actually care about their mom. Now, I think I'm starting to understand why they tried so hard last night to talk me into this. They adore her.

She slides a look my way. "Did Mason ever tell you how different things used to be for us?"

"No," I reply while her sons look like they're ready to choke.

"Mom, she doesn't want to hear about that," Mason informs her.

Like she cares. "It wasn't always like this. When I lost my John, they were only five and three years old. It was just the three of us after that. From as soon as they were old enough to earn money, they helped keep the lights on."

I can only imagine what they did to earn it, but she doesn't seem to think there was anything sketchy about it.

"It was too much for a couple of little boys, all that responsibility." She shakes her head with a sigh.

"We wanted to help you, Mom." Evan pats her shoulder, and I can't help but notice how his voice has changed. He's softer. Sweeter. "You never asked us to. It was our pleasure to take care of you after you took care of us all on your own."

She smiles lovingly at him. "When my health declined, they insisted on moving me into this fancy place. I get waited on hand and foot like I'm a queen. But no matter how many times I tell these two I don't need something so nice, they pretend they can't hear me."

"You deserve it." Mason kisses her cheek. "Just like you deserve all the presents." The three of them go through everything she received, folding sweaters and blouses, and putting the jewelry away.

They're just a family. I don't think I've ever felt this conflicted in my entire life.

"Excuse me." I stand and pick up the purse Mason bought me for today. "Where's the nearest restroom?"

"Out in the lobby, dear. When you get back, I want to hear all about how you two met." Mrs. Pavlis winks, and I give her a little smile before backing out of the room. Neither of the guys seems to notice I'm leaving. They're too busy going back and forth over whether Mom should have a safe in there with all this new jewelry.

I'm in the lobby before it hits me.

I'm alone. Finally. I don't know for how much longer, either.

I can go to the bathroom, or I can get out of here. The way my chest tightens at the thought of leaving Mason and Evan here is exactly why I have to go. What I saw from them back there in that room is almost enough to make me see them as whole people. Little boys who grew up in poverty without a dad. Who did what they had to do to take care of themselves and their mother. No wonder they turned out like they did, but they're still devoted to her.

Sorry, Mrs. Pavlis, but I can't live with your sons. Not if I want to avoid falling for them.

That's why I hurry through the front door without even bringing my jacket. It's freezing out, but I'm free. That's what matters. I have a little money in the bank, enough to afford a bus ticket somewhere. Anywhere.

I start jogging for the parking lot, hoping to reach the main road before anybody knows I'm gone. Maybe I can flag down a cop.

It's not until a black car skids to a stop in front of me that I realize I was never going to get away. I know even before the door opens and a man darts out to grab me and shove me inside that this was the way it was always going to end.

That it wouldn't be Evan or Mason who killed me. That it would be Dimitri.

"Hello again," he purrs once I'm inside, and his goon climbs in behind me. "Let's catch up."

"To the bathroom?" I look at Evan, who only scowls.

Mom shoots me a look. "What? You don't think women use the bathroom? I thought you knew better."

It's not easy to laugh it off. I go to the door, looking up and down the hallway, but don't see any sign of her. "I'll see if she's okay." I hear Mom murmuring something to Evan about it being cute, the way I care so much about Frankie. If she only knew.

Rapping on the door, I mutter, "You in there, Frankie?" For the sake of anybody who might be passing by, I keep my voice light. Inside it's another story. Inside I'm seething. I knew she'd pull something like this. I hoped she'd prove me wrong, though.

Finally, I turn to the front desk, where a cute little thing wears reindeer antlers on her head. "Excuse me, did a girl in a red sweater pass a minute or two ago?"

"Sure. She was in a hurry. I figured she left something in the car and would be right back since she wasn't wearing a coat."

She took the first opportunity and hauled ass. *Dammit, Frankie.* I go outside, searching, knowing I won't see her. She must've taken off at a run.

"Hey, Mom." I somehow manage to keep it together for her sake on returning to her room. "Frankie's not feeling well. I think we need to take her home." Evan doesn't say anything, but he puts on his coat and picks up Frankie's.

Mom's face falls. "Oh, no. I really wanted to get to know her better."

"We'll be back soon." I kiss her forehead and hope I didn't tell her a lie. Not that I haven't lied to her before, but this feels different. "I'm sorry to cut our visit short." Mom murmurs something vague about lunch in the dining room and movies in the entertainment center, so I don't think she'll be lonely.

Once we're outside, Evan blurts out what he's been holding back. "Motherfucker."

"I told you the tracker would come in handy." One of the errands Frankie didn't need to know about was picking up a tracking device that I then worked under the lining of her new sweater. She's not going anywhere without me being able to follow on my phone. By the time we reach the car, I have the app pulled up and working.

She's moving fast. Too fast to be on foot. "Where does she think she's going?" We stop at a light, and I hold the phone out for Evan to see.

"She's in a car. She got a ride."

"Somebody doing a good deed on Christmas Day or something else?" It only takes another moment or two of watching the blue dot's progress before I know exactly what happened. "He's got her. It's Dimitri. They're going straight to his club."

"How is that possible?"

"He followed us. I don't know, but it doesn't matter now." The closer the blue dot gets to the seedy section of down-town, the more certain I am. "I'll fucking kill him."

"Not if I get to him first." Evan hits the gas, rocketing the car down the freeway. Traffic's heavier than it would be on a normal weekday afternoon, but the BMW slides in and out with ease. Every second she's with him is one second closer to whatever Dimitri has planned. How much time passed between her running and us realizing she ran? A few minutes? Anything can happen in that stretch of time.

She's mine. Ours. It doesn't hit me until this moment how true it is. Even with only having spent a short amount of time together, I know she belongs to us. And we don't take well to anybody fucking with what's ours.

Surprisingly, Evan seems to feel the same since he is following her without question. We could just leave her with Dimitri and skip town. Instead, we're heading straight to his club.

Evan parks a couple of blocks down from the place. We get out of the car, heads on a swivel, and go to the trunk. Under the liner, we've stashed a couple of guns. I check two of them, making sure they're loaded before tucking both into my waistband. Evan does the same, then joins me as we head down the otherwise empty sidewalk. It's like a ghost town at this time of day.

There's no need to discuss a plan. We know what needs to be done.

Which is why we go through the alley and use the service entrance rather than knocking on the club's front door. He left it unlocked for us. Either he is that stupid, or he knew we'd come for her, and this is a trap. This is his way of killing two birds with one stone—getting Frankie out of the way and eliminating us for failing to complete the assignment.

Entering the kitchen, we find a pair of thick-neck thugs sitting at a prep table eating leftovers. They're too busy having lunch to notice us. I immediately fire on the one closest to me, and he falls backward off his stool and takes the plate of food with him.

"Not so fast." Evan's got the other one in his sights. The guy stops going for his weapon and raises his hands instead. "Where are they? Where did he take the girl?"

Before there's a response, a scream from somewhere in the building tells us she's on the second floor.

"No, no!" That's all Dimitri's guy manages to get out before Evan puts a bullet in his shoulder.

"Now." Evan takes him by the collar, hauling him to his feet. "You're gonna take us to her if you don't want a matching slug in your skull. Get it?" He keeps the muzzle pressed to the guy's temple while I disarm him, then shove him toward the doorway.

"I just work here, you know?" The guy smells like piss, and I realize he wet himself with fear. Of course, he did. A weak little pussy would hire guys weaker than himself, so he can feel superior. When he doesn't move fast enough, I shove him harder.

"Move, unless you want me to do to you what he's doing to her." That gets him practically jogging across the empty club. He unlocks a door set in the wall and leads us up a set of stairs so narrow we can only walk single file. It opens into a wide hall with a room at the end, the door half-open.

"His office," the guy whispers. I take him by the back of his collar and nudge him forward, standing behind him for cover. Evan's behind me, checking to make sure the other rooms are free of threats.

The door at the end of the hall suddenly swings fully open, and three armed men rush out. "Don't!" That's all the guy in front of me has time to shout before they pump lead into his gut. When the shooting slows—they must realize their mistake—Evan and I return fire until all three are on the floor.

I let the now-dead guard drop at my feet before continuing down the hall. Frankie's weeping loudly. The sound only intensifies my rage. "Don't hurt me anymore," she pleads as Evan and I approach, guns at the ready.

It's just the two of them. I see Frankie tied to a chair and take her in with a single glance: torn sweater, hair hanging in her face, bruises already forming on her bared shoulder. A handprint.

Dimitri's head snaps around when we enter. "What the—?"

A bullet to his knee makes him drop, screaming and clutching the spurting kneecap. It's one of the most painful places to be shot, but not deadly. I want this to last.

So does Evan, clearly. He steps up close to Dimitri and kicks him in the wounded knee. "How's it feel, fucker? Does it hurt?" Another kick makes Dimitri howl. There's already sweat rolling down his face.

I bend, taking a handful of greasy hair in one hand and yanking his head back. "You think you can hurt what belongs to us?"

"You accepted a job!" he bawls. "You were supposed to—"

I cut him off by shoving the muzzle of my gun into his mouth. "What's that? Did you want to say something?" Evan goes to Frankie and unties her. "What did he do to you?" I ask her.

She raises her head and reveals a bruise on her cheek. "He slapped me around and grabbed me a little. I'm okay." She's still weeping, trembling in Evan's arms, when he raises her from the chair. He envelops her, one hand cradling the back of her head.

"Nobody will ever hurt you again," he vows.

I jam the gun deeper into Dimitri's mouth, making him sob around the barrel. "You deserve every moment of agony you're going through, you sick fuck. A girl won't let you pimp her out, and you put a hit on her life?"

"This is nothing compared to what you deserve." Evan joins us, stepping on Dimitri's wounded knee until he shrieks.

I look up at Frankie, who's standing in the center of the room with her arms wrapped around her trembling body. "You shouldn't watch this," I warn.

She only stares at Dimitri, her eyes cold. "I want to." He whimpers, eyes wide, pleading to her without saying a word.

"Fair enough." I look at Evan, who shrugs before aiming for Dimitri's crotch and pulling the trigger.

His body jerks, his screams deafening. He cups himself with both hands, but blood pours from between his fingers anyway. "Thought you were hurting before?" I ask with a laugh. A glance at Frankie reveals her smirking satisfaction. She's not shaken by this at all.

Pride swells in my chest. Our girl is tougher than she looks.

We let him drag himself across the floor, leaving a trail of blood behind him until he curls up in the corner. "Please... need a doctor... oh, fuck!" He looks down at his blood-soaked crotch and hands, wailing in agony. "I'll fucking kill you for this!"

"Which is it? You want our help, or you want to kill us?" I stand beside my brother, who's as unbothered as I am. Dimitri's nothing but a bug who needs squashing. We should've done this from the beginning.

When we raise our guns, aimed at his head, he holds up his blood-covered palms. "Please, wait, wait! I'll give you anything you want!"

"You're right. You will," Evan confirms before we both pull the trigger. At least there's no more screaming.

I turn to Frankie, who's watched every second. Now she's trembling harder than ever. "Come on. We need to get her out of here." I sneer one last time at what's left of Dimitri before going to her, taking off my jacket and draping it over her shoulders.

"I'm sorry." Her eyes bulge when they meet mine. "I didn't mean to cause this."

"You didn't." Evan leads the way, watching for any strays we missed on the way up. It seems like the place is otherwise empty. I hurry Frankie past the bodies, noticing the way she gasps when she sees them. She doesn't say another word until we're away from the club, and I bundle her into the back seat before climbing in beside her.

"Is that it? Isn't somebody else going to come looking for you two?"

I pull her into my lap, then guide her head to my shoulder. She's safe. She's with us, and she's safe. "Don't worry about that. I didn't see any cameras, anyway."

"He wouldn't have wanted to record you in there with him," Evan points out. "Nobody will know it was us. He had plenty of enemies."

"I'm so sorry. I…" She shakes her head, her face pressed to my shoulder. When her shoulders start heaving, I can only hold her and stroke her hair, letting her cry it out on the way home. Right now, it's enough.

FRANKIE

"*Y*ou okay in there?"

Mason's on the other side of the closed bathroom door, having taken Evan's place a minute ago. They don't want to be too far from me, but it's not like before.

They understood when I said I needed a little time alone. All it took was getting kidnapped and watching them commit murder.

"I'm okay," I murmur, so he knows I didn't do something drastic. I have no intention of doing anything—not the way they think, anyway.

My skin will prune if I sit in the tub much longer, so I stand and drain the water before climbing out with a thick, fluffy towel wrapped around me. It's so luxurious. I still can't believe how comfortable I feel here... with them.

They came for me. They killed for me. For themselves, yes, but more to protect me. I know it. I feel it. And Mason holding me the whole way back? It was exactly what I needed.

They might be exactly what I need.

I dress in the satin nightie Mason bought me, another gift I didn't open last night when I was so hurt. It skims my thighs, hugging my curves. My nipples stand out against the black fabric. It's perfect.

I only hope I have the nerve to say what's in my heart when the time comes.

Mason's still waiting when I open the bathroom door. He and Evan took turns cleaning up, and now he's dressed in a gray tee and jeans. Even now, he looks good enough to make my stomach flutter. "Hey. I was wondering when you'd come out."

Then he notices what I'm wearing, and his eyes go round. "Oh. Fuck me."

That's sort of the idea. "Where's Evan?"

"Downstairs. He was going to heat last night's leftovers." His voice is sort of distant, softer than it should be, his

₎es taking me in a little bit at a time. My skin flushes from the attention.

"Let's go down. I want to talk to you both." I can do this. I have to do this. What's the worst that'll happen? If they turn me down, I'll go home. I can do that now. No more hit on me. No more Dimitri. Remembering that helps me lift my chin and gives me more confidence.

Evan is standing in front of the tree, the glowing lights making his black hair gleam. His reaction to me is close to Mason's, though he finds his voice easier. "You're fucking incredible."

I can only smile while my insides twist and turn. This is it. "I have something to say, and I have to get it out all at once, or else I'll lose my nerve." Now I wish I was wearing more clothes because I feel more exposed than ever. "I'm sorry I ran from you today, but I want you to understand why. It wasn't because I didn't want to be with you. It's because I did. I wanted to."

When all they do is frown at me, I shrug. "I was afraid. Being with you today, as a family, almost… it was nice. Too nice. I didn't want to start catching feelings for you two because of, you know, how things started out for us. You keep showing me these little bits of yourself, how sweet and thoughtful you can be, and that scared me. So I tried to run away. My heart wasn't really in it."

Somehow, I manage to take a deep breath. "I want to stay. I don't want you to send me home now that Dimitri is not after us. I know it's crazy, but I want to stay. I could take care of the house if you want. I'll earn my keep."

That seems to snap Evan out of it. "You think you'd have to work to earn your keep if you lived with us?" He glances at Mason, who only gapes at me. "Don't get me wrong. We'll put you to work. Just not the way you're thinking."

"We weren't about to send you home. Didn't you listen to anything we said before? You're ours." Mason moves toward me, shaking his head slowly. "You belong to us now."

I'm almost afraid to believe it's true. "You mean it? You still want me?" Evan comes up behind me and brushes my hair over one shoulder so he can kiss the other. "I thought... you hated..."

"I hated how unhappy you were." He kisses my shoulder again before caressing my neck with his lips. "That's all. Thinking I couldn't make you happy." I shiver when his hot breath hits my ear, and my legs threaten to go out on me. I have to lean back against him to support myself.

"There's no way we were going to let you go." Mason presses his body against mine, sandwiching me the way they did the first night together. Only this time, I admit liking it. His eyes stare deep into mine while his hands move up my thighs, working the satin higher. "Not now. Not ever. You belong with us. Always."

"Always," I whisper. He lowers his head, our breath mingling for a moment before our lips meet. It's sweet, tender, but still hot enough to make me moan when his tongue brushes mine.

Evan snakes a hand around my neck, breaking the kiss so he can turn my face to his. "Forever."

"Forever," I agree, and this time, he kisses me deeply, slowly, until wetness floods my pussy.

Mason sinks to his knees in front of me, nightie bunched up around my waist. He plants light kisses across the waistband of my panties before sliding them down and tossing them aside. I watch, transfixed by the sight of him closing his eyes and inhaling my scent like it's some precious perfume.

His tongue darts out, touching my slit, and I moan in approval. One of my hands sinks into Mason's hair while the other wraps around the back of Evan's neck. Evan's tongue trails down my throat, then up again while his arms slide around me so he can fondle my tits.

It's heaven. Pure bliss. Being worshipped and adored by men who'd kill to keep me safe. Who want me, always.

"That pussy belongs to us," Evan murmurs in my ear as Mason licks me. "Only us." He squeezes my tits, pinching the nipples, sending bolts of sizzling electricity through me.

"Yes… yes…" My head drops to his shoulder, eyes closed. I'd agree to anything right now. Mason moans against my pussy, grunting like a hungry animal as he eats me. All I can do is run my fingers through his hair and grind my hips against his face.

Evan chuckles darkly. "That's right. Ride his face. Take what you need before I take your ass, doll." I shiver at the thought and grind harder, more eager than ever to come. I want him that way. I want them both in any way they want to have me. They've already shown me part of myself I didn't know existed, the part that likes it rough and kinky. What else do I have left to learn?

Plenty. Like what it feels like to be slowly undressed before a leather belt is drawn around my wrists, hands behind my back. "What are you doing?" I ask, hazy and confused, as Evan suddenly turns me in place until I'm facing him.

He continues taking off his clothes while Mason guides me to my knees. "Getting ready for that ass." Evan drops his shorts, his cock springing free, close to my face. "Put it in your mouth."

I lean in cautiously with my arms behind me like they are. He guides himself between my lips before rolling his hips, plunging deep inside.

Mason spreads my legs until they're wide apart, which helps with my balance—and helps him drive his fingers up inside me. I find his cock rubbing against my lower back and manage to wrap a hand around it. "You hungry for this?" he rasps in my ear, fucking me with his fingers while he fucks my hand. I grip him tighter in response, and his groan sends goose bumps racing over my skin.

"Good girl." Evan strokes my hair while pumping into my mouth. "Keeping us nice and hard for you. I can't wait to feel you milking my cock." I suck in my cheeks, and his gentle hand turns into a fist, holding my head in place so he can let loose with a series of hard, sharp thrusts into the back of my throat.

It comes on all at once. The tightening around Mason's fingers, the tension building deep in my belly until there's nothing I can do but let go. Mason makes an approving sound, fingering me hard and fast, sending aftershocks shooting through me every time he rubs against my G-spot.

I barely know what's happening by the time I collapse against him, Evan's dripping cock swaying in front of me. He lowers me to the floor in a panting heap, still shivering as my climax fades away.

When Mason positions himself beside me, facing me, I want to reach out and grab him. I need the closeness, the connection, but my hands are tied. Evan's presence behind me helps ease the last of the trembling. "So fucking beautiful," he whispers in my ear, his fingers dancing over my thigh, my hip. He lifts my leg, draping it over Mason's thigh before running his cock between my ass cheeks.

"I've never... I don't..."

He kisses my shoulder, my neck, still lubing up my ass with the creamy remnants of my orgasm. "Shh, doll. I'll take it slow. You just relax now."

Mason turns my face to his and kisses me, his tongue probing mine, and soon there's nothing but pleasure again. Deep, sweet pleasure that goes on and on and only gets deeper when the pressure from Evan's head at my asshole unlocks sensations I've never imagined.

I tense up when he pushes inside, but Mason's kisses ease me back down again. Evan groans, frozen in place. "So fucking tight. Oh, my god…" He pushes in a little farther, and I moan into Mason's mouth. When his fingers brush my clit, I spread my legs wider to encourage him.

Though it isn't my clit he's interested in. Not really. More like my cunt, still dripping wet. He guides his cock to it, and my eyes fly open wide. I don't think I can handle this. I don't even think it's possible.

But it is. He enters me, and my eyes roll back in my head for a second as unthinkable pleasure threatens to break me in half. This is what I was meant for. This is who I was meant for.

They move together, only a thin wall separating their cocks. I'm lost, totally gone, my voice cracking and finally breaking, but I keep trying to cry out how incredible it feels. How much I want this. "Fuck me… please, fuck me…" I've never felt so connected, so right.

So damn good.

"Gonna come," Evan grunts, working in and out in time with Mason's thrusts. He groans his agreement, holding my leg high so he and his brother can take me hard. Fast. Deep.

It's building in me, too, starting from the place where we're connected. I can only close my eyes and hold on as they take me, using me to satisfy their needs while satisfying needs I didn't know I had. Rutting like animals, they're grunting and sweating against me, and it's all too much, it's too good, I can't—

"God, yes!" My shriek echoes off the walls and floor the instant before fireworks go off behind my eyelids. Evan buries his face in my hair and groans, hot cum flooding my ass and dripping out to mix with what Mason shoots up my pussy.

It's the sensation of their mixed juices running down my thighs that brings me back to reality, lying naked and panting between them. The Christmas tree lights make everything glow warm and bright—unless it's my joy making things seem that way. Maybe it's a little of both.

All three of us jump when a buzzer goes off in the kitchen. Evan laughs, disentangling himself from me. "I almost forgot dinner was in the oven."

"Good thing. We'll need sustenance if we're going to do that again before the night's over." Mason meets my gaze and flashes a naughty grin.

This is shaping up to be a very memorable holiday season indeed.

Thank you for reading The Christmas Mistake. Ready for another spicy Christmas read?
Check out Christmas Obsession *and keep reading for a preview...*

CHRISTMAS OBSESSION

Vincent

Walking into the kitchen, I allow myself a glance at my obsession. I catch her eyeing me curiously; something about the look in her eyes is strong but wary. The years with her selfish mother have not broken her spirit, but her soul is battered. She is innocent but wise, and she occupies my every thought.

I wish I could make her understand how special, how strong and brave she is. I wish I could do so much for her, have her by my side and give her anything she could ever want or need, but I can't. I can't have her.

I had to suppress a scoff when I enter the house to Margaret's boasting about her Christmas cookies as I hung my leather jacket on a coat rack. Instead of seeking out the girl I am really here for, I concentrated on holding back from calling Margaret out on her lies—that woman doesn't know how to bake a frozen pizza, let alone make cookies from scratch—and followed her into the kitchen.

Even if I hadn't already seen Faith making those cookies, I would've known Margaret is a liar. No one with hair that perfectly coiffed "just finished" making Christmas cookies. Margaret's desperation is nearly palpable, and perhaps in a past life, I would've humored her. Taken her to bed, then unceremoniously disappeared.

Ghosted, as my boss would say. But not anymore. I see through her lies, and it takes every ounce of control in my body to not scowl at her advances. But I play nice because this is my one chance.

The truth of the matter is that I'm not here for her. I'm here for Faith. Ever since I moved into the house next door, I've been watching her. It began with curiosity and ended in knowing every part of her life. I'm obsessed with knowing every little detail about her.

She attends the community college just down the road. She leaves for class at nine every morning and returns at five. Her favorite color is blue; she likes to read romance books and eat cookie dough ice cream. She listens to 70s rock albums in her car, on CD because she drives a fifteen-year-old sedan.

Meanwhile, her mother, Margaret, drives a Lexus and spends all her money on booze and clothes. She has enough money to send Faith to a nice college but chooses to waste her money on material, selfish things. It disgusts me. I want nothing more than to whisk Faith away from this small life and give her everything she deserves.

The more I learn about Faith, the more I know I have to protect her. Watch her, take care of her in any way I can. She is so small and fragile, she needs someone to look out for her, and her mother is doing a shit job.

Tonight is my only chance to see her up close. Then I'll go back to watching from afar. Back to yearning for the one woman, I can never have.

I live a life that she can never be a part of. Hitmen don't get to fall in love—especially not ones who work for the mafia. If I let her into my life, she would become collateral, a target, a weakness my enemies would use against me. If I drag her into my darkness, soil her lightness somehow, I would never forgive myself.

Besides, she would probably never go for me anyway. I am much older than her. I'm weathered, body and soul. She is young, full of light, and utterly innocent. We're the complete opposite, and there is no way she could ever see me for anything other than her neighbor.

I snap back to the moment, my eyes locking on Faith, standing there with a swipe of flour on her cheek. Her eyes are wide as if we've caught her in an indecent act.

Oh, if only...

"I just had to ask Faith to get the cookies out of the oven for me. She's such a great helper, aren't you, Faith?"

Margaret's tone is dripping with sugar. To me, it sounds like nails on a chalkboard. She never uses this tone for her daughter, only condescending whispers and harsh snarls.

I know because I haven't only watched them from my window. One day, while Faith and Margaret were out, I snuck into their house to plant two cameras in Faith's room. One points at her bed. One overlooks the rest of her room. Every night since then, I've watched her.

Yes, I'm a fucking stalker. Yes, it's wrong and perverted. It's completely immoral and devious, but I don't care. I'm going to hell anyway, might as well make it count.

Most of the time, she just reads, does homework, or sleeps. I watch the live feed obsessively, poring over her every movement. But I also watch when she touches herself. Those are my favorite parts.

She doesn't have any toys, no vibrators or massagers. She even masturbates innocently, with two fingers furiously rubbing at her swollen clit until she's gasping for air. It's almost primal. I shouldn't watch, but nothing else satisfies me. I must see her—all of her. She is my one and only obsession.

I set the cameras to record every time I leave the house, so I can come home and catch up with everything Faith has done that day. She spends most of her time at home in her room, but the windows in my home allow me to see into their living room and kitchen as well. That's how I'd seen Faith making these cookies before I came over.

I watch everything she does. *Everything.*

It's wrong. I know it is. But I'm addicted. She's a drug I cannot kick. I need her in every way, even though I know I cannot truly have her.

That's what makes it so surreal to be standing in the same room as her. To smell the cookies, she'd made just for me. To know what she looks like naked, what she sounds like when she comes on her hand, but to have to introduce myself as if are strangers. Which, to her, we are. She has no idea how much I know about her. How much I want to unravel her, to strip her bare and taste her sweetness, to feel her beneath my body, my cock sliding into her, bringing her to the brink of orgasm again and again.

"Hello, Faith," I greet, my voice low as I fight to keep my heartbeat even.

Oh, sure, I could assassinate enemies of the mob without a second thought, but saying hello to her makes me nervous? Of course, it fucking does. I don't want her to know about the darkness that lives inside of me. The joy I get from killing people, the warmth of their blood on my hands, listening to their screams, and pleas.

Faith turns to face me, and I watch a blush creep across her cheeks. So fucking beautiful. I want to kiss her, to spread her out right here on the counter, and claim her as mine.

"Hi, Vincent. Merry Christmas," she replies shyly, her blue eyes flicking away from me almost nervously. It takes everything in me not to step closer.

You aren't good enough for her. Too dark. Too dangerous.

Luckily, I don't have to stop myself because Margaret forces herself between us. She clings to my arm for a moment as she snaps at her daughter.

"Christmas *Eve*, Faith. It's not Christmas yet." She's trying to sound like she's playfully teasing, but I hear the edge in her voice.

Margaret turns back to me with a winning smile, pushing up her chest in hopes that I'll get lost in her vast cleavage. I don't fall for it, not when the only woman in the room who has my attention is Faith.

"Does it really matter, Mom?" Faith shoots back.

I hate watching the expression of hurt appear on her face and nearly throw Margaret off of me. But instead, I gently lift her hands from my arms and move her to the side. Margaret stands dumbly, unsure how to react to me rejecting her advances, as I step forward.

"Pardon me for wanting to be accurate," Margaret huffs.

She turns on her black stiletto heels—I wonder what type of woman willingly wears them in her own home—to open up a cabinet on the other side of the room. "Let me grab a serving tray, and we'll have these cookies."

While Margaret busies herself, I move closer to Faith. From here, I can smell her, the sugar cookies, and vanilla, all things sweet, wafting from her body. My mouth waters, and all I want to do is take a bite out of her. Her scent is intoxicating, enough to bring me to my knees.

She's wearing a sweet sweater and tight black leggings. I can see the gentle curve of her ass, and almost stop breathing when she stands on her tiptoes and leans over the counter, giving me a perfect view of her sculpted legs. All I want is to hoist her over my shoulder and take her back to my house, where I can finally make her mine.

Stop! I can't...

"You've made some wonderful cookies," I whisper under my breath as I grab a sweater-shaped cookie. Faith straightens and looks at me in shock, like she can't believe I'm complimenting her on the cookies I know she made.

Her blue eyes go as wide as saucers, and being this close to her, I notice that there's a smattering of freckles across her nose. My stomach tenses, and I feel like an animal. I lock eyes with her as I bite into the cookie, letting the sweetness dance across my tongue.

Damn. It tastes amazing. Faith is an incredible baker, and just when I thought she couldn't be any more perfect.

"Oh, I uh. No, it's okay. My mom did—" she stammers.

I understand why she lies for her mom, but it pains me.

"I know the truth, Faith. Don't worry." I wink. It's the only advance I'll allow myself to make at her. I'll behave the rest of the night, not because I want to, but because I have to.

Margaret pops between us with a garish plastic serving dish patterned with holly leaves. She pretends to be shocked when she sees that I've taken a bite already. It's overdone, as if she's an actress on stage, playing to the back row. In close quarters, it's annoying and insincere.

"Vincent! Tut, tut," she says, playfully slapping me on the hand. "You just couldn't wait to help yourself to my baking, could you? Well, I surely don't blame you. But let's go start up the fireplace, hmm?"

Margaret struts off toward the living room, and I motion for Faith to go ahead of me.

"After you," I say with a small wave.

She smiles at me from beneath a strand of hair on her face, and before I can stop myself, I wipe that stripe of flour off of her cheek. She lets out a soft gasp when my thumb makes contact with her face but maintains eye contact while her face turns red-hot.

She smiles again but quickly turns away, following her mother. I keep pace close behind, keeping my eyes on the back of her head. Wouldn't want Margaret to catch me staring at her daughter's ass. I must keep some semblance of decorum.

Margaret sits on the couch with one leg crossed over the other. Her green dress has ridden up enough that I can see the lace garter of her pantyhose. Faith must notice too because she gives a hefty eyeroll as she flops into the easy chair facing the couch. Margaret is patting the cushion beside her, but I decline and sit on the opposite arm of the couch, leaving one seat between us.

A friendly evening between neighbors. That's all this is.

Find Christmas Obsession on Amazon.

ABOUT THE AUTHOR

Darcy Rose is a USA Today Bestselling author of steam novellas with a dark edge.

If you like your books short, taboo and kinky, then you have come to the right place. Darcy writes about shy and innocent heroines, to match them up with dark and intense heroes who have only eyes for one girl.

STANDALONES

Christmas Obsession

The Christmas Mistake

Extra Credit

Heaven

Twice the Hate

Twice the Temptation

Made in the USA
Coppell, TX
06 December 2021